"IF YOU WAS SMART, YOU WOULDN'T MESS WITH ANOTHER MAN'S WOMAN."

Slocum looked around in mock surprise. "I mess with your woman, Walker? I apologize."

There was laughter from the porch at that. Walker glared at the men watching and then at Slocum. "You know who I mean. Miss Dory is Sam Boldt's property. Don't nobody lay a hand on his property when I'm around. That's my job."

"You ain't too good at it, then. I heard somebody snatched Boldt's bride for ransom. Where were you then? Or is your job only shooting off your mouth?"

Walker moved out into the dust of the street. "You take that gun off, and I'll show you what my job is."

Slocum shrugged and stepped into the dust. He had no other choice and unbuckled his gunbelt, placing it on the porch. Walker was on him before he'd even turned around....

JAKE LOGAN

THE CANYON BUNCH

BERKLEY BOOKS, NEW YORK

1

Two hours after he landed in Bowie, John Slocum found himself in jail.

Bowie came in sight at around noon of a hot day; he rode down out of the hills to the north and saw it five or six miles ahead, set out by itself on a hot, baked plain. It didn't look like much, and what he saw when he got closer was no improvement: one block of weathered buildings flanking a dusty street in the blistering sun, the street itself merely part of a road stretching away to the east and west, toward horizons as treeless as the town. It wasn't a place he would have stopped in, but he was looking for a friend named Red Wylie, and Bowie was where Red had last been heard from.

In the blaze of noon, the town looked deserted. He stabled his horse, a long-legged gray he'd bought before leaving Oregon, and carried his war bag along the unshaded boardwalk till he found a barbershop, run by a Chinaman, and got himself a shave. Shorn of his beard, his hair cut for the first time in a month, he rented a tub in the back room and sat in it for close to an hour, occasionally calling for the barber to pour another bucket of hot water over him. A night in a hotel bed would be a welcome change; after that he would set about finding Red. If Red was still alive.

He was standing in the tub, toweling himself off, when the door opened and a man came in carrying a shotgun, a tin star pinned to his vest. He was tall and lanky, with flecks of gray in his handlebar mustache. He took Slocum in at a glance, then propped one boot on the chair where Slocum had left his clothes and gun belt, the shotgun laid across his knee, pointing toward the tub, his finger on the trigger.

"You John Slocum?" he said.

"I generally knock before I come in on a man taking a bath," Slocum said.

"You just ride in? That your gray gelding in the livery stable?"

Slocum finished toweling himself off and stepped out onto the board floor. He had one eye on his gun belt, but that chair was at least ten feet across the room, and it wasn't smart to tackle a man with a shotgun. "Suppose I said I wasn't?"

"Then I'd have to call you a liar. Tom Watson at the stable gave me a good description of you. And you're the first stranger this town's seen in a month."

"I wouldn't want a man calling me a liar. What's it to you who I am?"

"The name's Brady. I'm town marshal." He lifted Slocum's Colt from its holster, shoved it in his waistband, and backed off toward the door, bringing the shotgun up. "I'm going to have to throw you in my jail."

Slocum glanced toward the window in the back wall, beyond which he could see a few scattered buildings and the slope of a little hill covered with greasewood and sage. He would never make it through that window, and there was nothing he could do if he did, naked as he was.

"You mind telling me what for?"

"Watson says he recognized you. Says he was in Virginia City when you and some other boys held up a bank there. Says there's a warrant out for you, and a good-sized reward."

"Civic-minded citizen, is he? Or just greedy?" Slocum crossed to the chair and began putting on his clothes. "You're wasting your time. If there was a reward on my head, I'd be the first to know it. And I don't know it."

"If that's so, you got nothing to worry about. But pick ten men drifting alone across this country, the law will be looking for nine of 'em. So you'll just sit in my jail while I look through my 'Wanted' circulars. Maybe I'll hit pay dirt."

Slocum stamped his heels down into his boots and stood up to put his shirt on. He didn't think the marshal would find anything. It was true there was a warrant out for him in a place or two between the Mississippi and the Rockies, but none, so far as he knew, in this particular territory. It was likely the liveryman had seen him somewhere or other—he had crossed a lot of paths in the last few years—but he had never held up a bank in Virginia City. Some other places, maybe, but not Virginia City.

He slung the empty gun belt over his shoulder and picked up his war bag. "All right, let's get it over with."

Outside, he started west along the boardwalk, the marshal following close behind. The town still looked deserted, the streets empty. Except for a storekeep visible through a window here and there, the buildings looked the same. Not much of a town for Red Wylie to have settled in, if this was where he was. According to Red's family, in Oregon, his last letter had come from Bowie, Nevada, but that had been three years ago. A drifter like Red might already have moved on. And it would be hard to find a man if you were locked up in a cell.

They had reached the jail, a one-story adobe building set on the west end of town. The door stood open into a small office with a row of three cells across the back. The marshal prodded Slocum inside and took a ring of keys off a nail on the wall.

"You go in there," he said, and swung open the door to a cell just behind his cluttered desk. "Leave the war bag and the gun belt out here."

Slocum stepped into the cell, the door clanged shut,

and the key turned in the lock. Only bars separated the cells from the office, and with nothing to shield a prisoner from watching eyes, he would have no chance to dig his way out. There was a barred window high up on the wall, but it was too small to crawl through. If the marshal found his face on one of those "Wanted" circulars, he was going to be in trouble.

Brady took a seat at his desk, hiking his chair half around so he could keep an eye on Slocum. He removed a bottle and a glass from a bottom drawer and poured himself a drink. Then he opened another drawer and took out a stack of circulars three inches thick.

"This may take a while, so you better get comfortable."

"I don't suppose you'd want to share some of that bottle," Slocum said.

"No, I wouldn't," Brady said, and started leafing through the circulars.

Slocum sat down on the bunk and propped himself against the wall, examining what he could see of the jail. A rifle rack stood in one corner of the office, an iron bolt locked across it. There was a chamber pot under the bunk in each cell, and a broom in a corner of his own—evidently a prisoner was expected to keep his own floor swept. The chamber pots were mercifully empty and clean; the cells looked like they'd been vacant for quite a while. Hard to see that there was much need for a jail in a town this size. Likely cowhands came in on a Saturday night, and some of them would sober up here before the boss paid for whatever windows or street lamps they'd shot out. He wondered if Red Wylie had spent any time in this cell. From what he'd heard, Red had been in more than one jail since he had seen him last.

That had been seventeen years ago, in Georgia, in '65, when being on the losing side of the war had turned a lot of men bad. Slocum had lost the family place to carpetbaggers, and Georgia didn't seem a good place to stay, being picked clean as it was by the

Yankee occupation. With only defeat to look back on, little to look forward to, and nothing to lose, Red and Slocum had put together a band of ex-Rebels and led a raid on a Union army payroll train. They hadn't got away with much, but enough to carry them out of Georgia: Slocum to Texas, and Red with his daddy and his brother to Oregon. There had been a few letters exchanged over the years, so when Slocum had found himself in Oregon a few months back, he knew where to find the Wylies. Red's brother had a family and a farm up in the Willamette Valley, but Red had never settled down, they said; he had come back out here to the wild country. And Red's daddy was getting old and wanted him home. A man didn't want to die knowing there was bad blood between him and his son.

It never mattered much to Slocum where he rode—one place was as good as another—so he had agreed to look Red up and bring him the message: Blood was blood, even if it had turned bad, and his daddy wanted to make it good before he died.

But Red had to be found first, and that meant getting out of this jail.

The sun was low in the west and slanting in along the floor when the marshal finally sighed and returned the last circular to the pile. He pushed the pile aside and poured some more whiskey in his glass.

"You're in luck," he said. "I got nothing on you."

"I won't say I told you so. But likely that liveryman thought I was somebody else." Slocum swung off the bunk and went to stand at the bars.

The marshal drank off the whiskey and put the bottle back in the drawer. "Don't consider yourself too lucky. I've got no warrant on you, but it wasn't somebody else Tom Watson thought you were. He knew your name. I maybe can't hold you now, but if I see you take one step out of line, you'll be back in that cell so fast you'll think you never left it. There's been too many drifters collecting around this town lately. So if you're smart you'll leave this country while you can."

When the cell was unlocked, Slocum retrieved his Colt and strapped his gun belt on. "You give me some help," he said, "and maybe I can leave this country fast enough to suit both of us. I'm looking for a man named Red Wylie. Supposed to be living around Bowie somewhere. You know where I can find him?"

"If he's in Bowie, I don't know him, but I only been marshal here a month. If he's an honest man, maybe he rides for one of them cow outfits down south. If he's another drifter, he could be hanging out with that rough crowd in the canyons west of town. Samuel Boldt would know. He knows most everything around here. As a matter of fact, he owns most everything around here."

"Fine. Where can I find him?"

"Boldt lives in the Drover's Hotel, halfway up the block on this side of the street. He owns it. But you won't find him there today. He was set to get married next month, and some of that canyon crowd went and abducted his bride two days ago. Holding her for ransom. Sam's out trying to locate where they took her. He ought to be back tonight, though."

"A low bunch that would steal a woman for ransom. He know who did it?"

"Nobody knows for sure. Man named Ashe Greene, most likely. He's collected the kind of hardcases out there that would do such a thing. And if your friend is in on that, he's looking to get himself hanged. Maybe you ought to just ride on and forget about him."

"Maybe I better talk to Samuel Boldt," Slocum said, and hoisted his war bag onto his shoulder.

"Remember, one step out of line, and you're right back in that cell."

Outside, the sun was throwing long shadows up the empty street. Slocum carried his war bag along the boardwalk, heading for the sign that said THE DROVER'S

HOTEL. If Samuel Boldt owned it and lived there, it was likely a fancy place, but he'd been riding a long time and he deserved a room in a good hotel. And he wanted to get next to Boldt, and the Drover's Hotel would be the place to do it.

He didn't like the sound of what Brady had told him. From what the Wylies had said, Red had spent the last few years drifting farther and farther away from the law, and if Red was around here, he wouldn't be riding herd for forty a month on some cow spread to the south. Most likely he was out there in the canyons working for a man named Ashe Greene, riding herd on a scared woman stolen for ransom. And if that was true, there was less chance of getting him home to his family than there was of seeing him dance at the end of a hangman's rope.

2

The Drover's Hotel was a big two-story building halfway down the block, with a high wide porch across the
front. Slocum carried his war bag inside and set it down
at the front desk.

The place looked fancy enough—Bowie must draw
more trade from the surrounding territory than he'd
figured. The clerk's desk was on the right, just inside
the door, in front of a little closed-off cubicle. A mahogany bar ran along the wall on the left, a barkeep in a
white shirt and tie polishing glasses under a long stretch
of mirror. Chandeliers hung from the ceiling, and ranks
of cloth-covered tables filled the back of the room.
Through an entranceway at the far end of the bar, he
could see into an adjoining room, where there was a
roulette wheel and tables for faro and poker. He figured
Boldt would have a stable of women working the place
on a busy night, the women and the gambling tables all
bringing money into Boldt's till. No wonder that canyon bunch thought it a smart move to hold his bride-to-
be for ransom.

He rented the cheapest room he could get—five dollars a night—and carried his war bag across the thin,
patterned carpet toward a sweeping staircase behind the
clerk's cubicle. A blond woman in a low-cut gown,
playing solitaire at one of the tables, gave him an
inquisitive glance as he started up the stairs.

The place might be fancy, but the room was like any
other he'd stayed in in cow towns from Texas to Kan-
sas: bleak and small, with a chifforobe, a dresser, an
iron-railed bed, and flowered wallpaper faded to the

color of dust. Through the chintz curtains at the window he could see the late sun on a set of cattle pens out back. He changed into fresh clothes from his war bag, went back downstairs, and ordered himself a meal.

Sunlight fell on the tables through big windows in the rear wall. The town seemed just as quiet as when he'd ridden in; the woman playing solitaire was the only other person in the room. He figured her for one of Boldt's working girls—she had that look about her, and she kept darting glances at him as if trying to stir up a little business on a slow afternoon. He had just finished his meal and was wondering if he could afford a woman in a place like this when the bartender came over with a drink.

"Compliments of the lady."

Slocum glanced across the room in surprise. She was threading her way through the tables toward him, carrying a drink of her own. That surprised him too; usually even a saloon woman liked a man to make the move after she had given him the come-on.

The bartender had gone discreetly back to the bar. The woman halted beside Slocum's table, faint traces of amusement at the corners of her mouth. "Welcome to Bowie," she said.

She was maybe thirty, her blond hair curled close around her ears, and no bigger than five-one or five-two, but the cut of her gown showed that what she lacked in height she made up for in amplitude. Her breasts swelled out big and round above a tiny waist, and just by looking he could tell her skin would be smooth to the touch, sleek and fine as satin. The gown was snug around her hips, showing power just waiting to be unleashed, and the skirt was slit up to about mid-thigh, the ruffled edges of the slit parted just enough to reveal a well-rounded leg. He glanced from her little high-heeled shoes to her face and found her grinning at him, a mischievous glint in her eyes.

"You mind if I sit down?"

"Sorry." He rose to pull out a chair for her. "I guess you took me by surprise."

Seated, she saluted him with her glass. "Here's to surprises."

"I'll drink to that."

He felt the whiskey burn down inside him, adding to the heat generated by that pleased look on her face. He'd been a long time without a woman, and this looked to be one who enjoyed the line of work she was in. She kept pushing that provocative grin at him, those mischievous eyes locked on his.

"You keep looking at me like that," she said, "and we'll end up embarrassing Ray Petty there behind the bar."

"Didn't know it was that obvious," he said, and forced himself to stop looking at her breasts.

"You been looking at me ever since you walked in. That kind of look does things to me. And sometimes sitting around idle all day gets me so I want to go find me a bull in one of them holding pens outside. What do you say we go upstairs?"

Her directness made his mouth go dry; he had to swallow just to speak. "Not sure I can afford it. You look like luxury off the top shelf to me."

She grinned and cocked her head at him. "That's not a business proposition. I wouldn't charge you."

Slocum downed his drink and got to his feet, watching her legs flash in the slit of the skirt as she rose to join him. He was about to ask why he was being specially favored when the bartender came over to the table.

"You sure you know what you're doing, Dory?"

"Ray," she said, "suppose you just mind your own business."

"That's what I am minding. You know my business ain't just tending bar."

"Well, suppose you go back and mind that part of your business. I'll worry about the rest of it."

Slocum followed her up the stairs and along the second-floor hallway, watching her tight round rump working inside the snug fit of the gown. "What was that all about?"

"Oh, just Ray butting in on my affairs. He thinks he has to keep an eye on me." She opened a door off to the left of the hall and led him inside.

The windows in the far wall looked out onto the cattle pens in back, but it was nothing like the room the clerk had given him. It was about three times the size, and the bed—a four-poster with a canopied top—was big enough for four people to sleep in. The coverlet was made out of some sort of satiny material, dyed a scarlet so bright it nearly hurt his eyes. A glass-doored chiffo-robe stretched halfway across one wall, and he could see into a kind of sitting room through a door beyond the bed.

"Wouldn't you rather look at me?" she said.

He turned to see her working on the buttons at the back of the gown, arms akimbo, watching him with that provocative grin. She loosed the last button, and the gown fell away to her waist. She wore nothing underneath it.

The sight of her took his breath away. Her breasts, cantilevered out over her rib cage, were even bigger than he'd suspected. The nipples were already erect, large and pink. She straightened up and started squirming the gown down over her hips, her breasts jiggling.

"You want to help me undress?"

"The hell with that," he said, and went to scoop her up off the floor, heading for the bed.

She giggled, kicking the gown loose from around her legs. He heard one high-heeled shoe hit the floor, then the other, and she was naked in his arms, hands clasped around his neck, pulling his mouth down to hers so that he had to set her down blind on the bed. He was out of his clothes in less time than it took to think, and on the bed with her, in her, her legs going up around his waist, her hands sliding up his ribs to grip him just below his shoulders.

He sank deep into her, propped on hands and knees on the bed, the sight of her voluptuous body naked on the scarlet coverlet beneath him so enticing he. was unable to restrain himself, rearing back and lunging, pile-driving, hot and fast; but she did something with her legs, stiffened her back in some way that brought him hard up against the engorged roof just inside her, the pressure from her legs and from the way her body was arched forcing him to slow, making each gather-and-thrust long and powerful, slow out and slow in, keeping him at the pace she wanted, her eager eyes watching his face, that pleased provocative grin never leaving her mouth.

He felt half drunk, his hips rocking in long slow thrusts into her, watching every thrust reverberate through her, her big breasts jiggling, erect nipples pointing up at him. He seemed trapped just below release, on the edge of climax, and each time he lunged up toward it, thinking it within reach, he met some trick she had that kept him right there, right on that edge. And then he adjusted to it, knew that it was going to last, that with this woman he could make it last. He felt her fingernails rake down across his ribs, saw her grin widen to a pleased leer as he jerked in response; and despite even that, he knew he could take her, bring her right up to where he was, where it so pleased her to have sent him: hot and blood-brained and half drunk with lust.

The thought seemed to give him new power; he slid one arm around under the small of her back, bringing her up off the coverlet till only her shoulders touched the bed, her legs around his waist, and he got control of the pace then, broke the hold of her body and began thrusting deep into her, long and slow and powerful, feeling that hot drunken lust raging through his brain, driving and driving into her until he saw her eyes go closed, saw her hands come down to clutch at the coverlet, saw her head begin to rock from side to side, her lower lip caught between her teeth. And then the little cries began to come from her; he felt her ankles lock across his back; her hands clutched the coverlet for leverage, and her hips began pumping frantically; but for a moment he held her to that long slow pace she had held him to before, never losing contact with that rough blood-engorged roof just inside her; then he loosed the restraint and felt her surge into wild rapid lunging.

He caught up to her pace, surpassed it, mastered it, mastered her, his own eyes going closed from the heat of it, hearing now in the dark of his own drunkenness the wild cries piercing the room as she surged up in a wild frantic rhythm that brought her up and over, him coming after her, lunging and thrashing in a long final frenzy that brought them both back down on the bed. He felt her hands snake up around his neck, felt those big breasts heaving against his chest, felt her shudder up against him, shudder down again, and then leech herself to him in one final prolonged quiver, all her sleek round curves soft against his skin.

They lay that way for what seemed a long time, on their sides, her head tucked down under his. He was still in the warm hollow of her thighs, her legs around his waist. He cupped the nape of her slim neck, feeling consciousness slowly returning. A faint breeze stirred the curtains at an open window. He could tell the sun was just setting outside. And now he became aware of the clatter and bawling of cattle—a herd being driven into the holding pens just beyond the window.

After a while she pulled away, eyes regarding him with a kind of gentleness he hadn't seen in her before. "There's not many men can do that to me. Make me lose myself like that." Then she grinned and slid a sharp fingernail up his chest. "But you and me, we always were good together."

He rose to one elbow, surprised. "You and me? Do we know each other?"

That mischievous look returned to her face, drowning out the gentleness. "You don't remember me, do you, Johnny Slocum? I oughta be mad at you for that. But somehow I can't be mad right now." She rolled off the bed and crossed to a cabinet, her round little rump twitching from side to side. She tossed him a towel, then returned to kneel on the bed beside him. "I thought sure you'd remember them times we went night-swimming back in Georgia in '65."

He sat all the way up on the bed, awestruck, memory flooding into him. "Well, I'll be damned," he said. "Dory Baker."

"You do remember, don't you?" She leaned over to kiss him, big breasts swinging heavily. "That makes up for it."

It was like taking him back to his youth. He remembered her round little face now, the high cheekbones and the mischievous eyes, and that cheeky grin she'd always had. And the times she'd sneaked out of her daddy's house in the dead of night, creeping in her flannel nightgown down across the lean-to roof below her window to ride behind his saddle to the river at the back of the field behind the house. Night-swimming, she'd always called it, though very little swimming went on back there, unless you could call swimming what they did on the blanket under the trees beside the river. She'd been just a kid then, barely into her teens. He hadn't been much more than a kid himself, though he'd already had four years of war behind him, four years of mud and blood and minié balls, years of seeing the big gray armies dwindle down to nothing, of seeing the cause he'd believed in go down.

She was still grinning at him. "I woulda thought you'd remembered me better than that. I remembered you."

"That was a long time ago, Dory. Seventeen years ago. Besides, I don't remember you being quite so big." He reached out to palm one big breast. "Up here, I mean."

She giggled and looked down at her breasts, sliding her hands up to cup the heavy weight of them. "I was just starting to fill out then. I filled out real good that next year, after Red and me got to Oregon."

He remembered her even then as a provocative little thing, but she could be demanding, too, and distracting, and he had been right in the middle of planning the raid on that Yankee payroll train, trying to hold together a disgruntled bunch of ex-Rebs to pull it off with, so he had broken off with her. Red had taken up with her then, and when they'd all had to flee Georgia, after hitting the train, she had talked Red into taking her with him.

"I should have known I'd find you wherever I found Red. Red always was stuck on you."

"Red's been tagging after me ever since we left Georgia. I wanted to stop in some of these towns out here, where the boom was going and you could do pretty much what you pleased. But Red, he begged and begged till he got me to go to Oregon with him. And Oregon was about as exciting as a turtle race. So I found me a man wanted to come back to this country, and I left."

"And Red followed you."

"Been following me for fifteen years. He'll hang around till I get tired of him and drive him off. Then he'll head back to Oregon, or someplace else. But first thing you know, he'll be back, and he'll find me. Red's sweet, you know, but he ain't much of a man. He gets worse every year—bitter, I guess. Life ain't turned out like Red thought it would. He's hanging around with a pretty rough bunch now, out in the canyons west of town. Rustling stock off those cow outfits down south is what the rumor says."

"And stealing Sam Boldt's bride-to-be for ransom?"

She examined his face. "You heard about that? I don't know as Red's in on that. I don't really know where he is now. There's several bunches hole up out in them canyons, and they move around a lot.''

"Well, I told his family I'd send him home to Oregon. The marshal told me Boldt might know where he is. I take it you know Boldt. You must, working here.''

"I don't work here. Not anymore. But sure, I know Sam. Better than anybody.'' She grinned at him—cocky, proud—and looked around to take in the canopied bed, the expensive fabrics, the big sofa just visible in the adjoining room. "Who do you think pays for all this?''

It dawned on him then: Dory Baker was Sam Boldt's woman. Or at least one of them. "I thought he was fixing to get married.''

"He is. Or was before Ramona got abducted. That don't mean he can't keep me on the side. I've known him longer than she has. I bet she can't do what I can, make him feel good like I can. And Ramona Warren's no better than me. She met him working downstairs, same as I did.''

"You mean she's a whore? Boldt's marrying one of his whores?''

"A lot of men out here find themselves a wife in a place like this. There's nothing wrong with it.''

He realized he'd just barely avoided calling Dory a whore herself, though that was clearly what she was, even as Boldt's private woman. He'd always suspected she would end up a whore, even back in '65, when she'd told him she would never let herself get tied down by marriage, that she aimed to live her own life, no matter what it took. Knowing the kind of woman she was, likely she'd set out deliberately to become a whore. It seemed to suit her. And now some other woman out of Boldt's stable had persuaded him to marry her. That surely couldn't have made Dory happy, but she wasn't letting any displeasure show.

She was still kneeling on the bed; now she started stroking her breasts, watching him with that cocky grin as her fingers plucked at her nipples, pulling them up and out, so that her breasts jiggled heavily when she released her hold. "You like the way I filled out since you seen me last?"

"Be a strange man that didn't."

"I always wanted to be big on top." She looked down at herself, lifting those large breasts in her palms. "For a long time I was afraid they weren't going to get big."

The sight of her was beginning to bring him up again. She looked down at the proof of it, giggled, and plopped down beside him, running a hand up his flank.

"I see the years ain't slowed you down none."

"Maybe a little," he said.

But she was already hiking one leg up over his hip, pulling him in between her thighs, and then he was in her again, and moving; and this time it was slower, gentler, she clinging to his waist, her eyes closed, and him reared back a little so he could take in the sight of those jiggling breasts, her nipples erect, her hips writhing in slow ecstasy, her breathing quickening till she surged up over that peak of pleasure and he let himself follow after.

She cuddled up in his arms then, while he stroked the smooth skin of her back and watched the sun fade outside the window. He could still hear the bawling of the cattle in the holding pens. He didn't remember her being this gentle back in Georgia. She had been feistier then, those nights down by the river more like the way a couple of angry cats might have gone at it than like two people making love. Maybe life had taught her a thing or two, the way it did everybody. He couldn't help feeling a little bad that his prediction had come true, that she'd ended up a whore, though it didn't seem to bother her. Maybe it was what she'd wanted.

He could tell by her breathing that she was asleep. He pulled away from her gently as he could, rose from the bed, and went to the window. The sun had gone down; outside was the stillness of early evening. The cattle had quieted some, bunched up near the center fence of the holding pens. Two cowhands sat on a rail, spitting tobacco juice and talking. The rest of them had probably headed for one saloon or another.

He cleaned himself up, dressed, and took one last look at Dory. She was sleeping still, bare as a baby on the scarlet coverlet, her knees drawn up, arms cradled over her breasts. She even looked like a baby, curled up like that, with a little childish pout on her face. He half expected to see her thumb in her mouth.

Sam Boldt might be back by now. He figured he would go down and see if the man could tell him where to find Red Wylie.

3

The saloon was no longer empty. Several dusty cow-hands were gathered at the bar, evidently the bunch that had brought those cattle into the holding pens behind the hotel. Drinks were being bought by a windburned middle-aged gent in a sweat-stained Stetson, probably the trail boss or the owner of the herd. The chink of coins rang on the bar top through the hum of talk and laughter. Slocum sidled to the near end of the bar, away from the others, and ordered a whiskey.

The bartender set it in front of him and took a swipe at the mahogany with his cloth. "You're in trouble, friend."

He said it low, but Slocum was suddenly aware that the noise had subsided and that he was being watched by the men along the bar.

"Is that right?" he said.

"That woman you took upstairs. She belongs to Samuel Boldt. Mr. Boldt owns this place, and he don't like other men messing with his property."

Slocum took a sip of his whiskey. Now he understood the barely stifled grins on the men watching. "That didn't seem to bother her," he said. "It bother you?"

"Not me. My job's just to keep an eye on her. Dealing with the situation is somebody else's job."

Slocum scanned the faces along the bar. "Do I have to guess which one?"

"He's waiting for you outside. Matt Walker." The bartender glanced at the way Slocum's holster was tied down to his thigh. "You may be fast with that Colt.

23

That'll do you no good. Matt don't wear a gun. He's a very big man, and he likes to force a man to meet him on his own ground. With his fists.''

"Suppose you tell Sam Boldt I'm here," Slocum said. "I'd prefer to discuss any differences with the boss.''

"Mr. Boldt is out of town.''

So Boldt hadn't come back yet. Dory must have known this would happen. The Dory he remembered would have enjoyed seeing two men fight because of her. There was no reason to believe seventeen years would have made her any different.

Everybody was watching him. He knew he had to go out, had to face this Matt Walker or leave town right now. There were still things he wanted to do in this town and backing down was a bad habit he didn't want to start. He drank off the whiskey and shoved the glass across the bar.

He saw Matt Walker as soon as he came out through the bat-wing doors. The man was leaning against a porch support at the bottom of the steps, rummaging at his teeth with a toothpick. The bartender hadn't lied: Walker wore no gun, and he was very big, with massive shoulders and long arms. His feet alone looked big enough to kick a hole through a wall. Only one thing was encouraging: He didn't look too bright; he had the big stupid face of a mastiff, of a man who would bull his way through a fight but wouldn't be too clever at it. That was something, anyway.

From the corner of his eye, Slocum saw several oldsters sitting in chairs tipped back against the wall of the hotel. People were drifting out of doorways across the street, not bothering to disguise their interest. He could sense the men from the saloon crowding up at the bat-wing doors behind him. Likely watching Matt Walker in a fight was what this town did for sport.

No sense waiting. He left the door and started down the steps past Walker.

Walker made his move then. He lurched out from the porch support as if to start across the street and collided with Slocum as he passed, knocking him backward along the bottom step. Slocum righted himself to see Walker glaring at him, ham hands dangling like those of an ape.

"Why don't you watch where you're going?" Walker said.

"You were watching close enough. I figured I'd let you worry about it."

"You got a smart mouth, mister. But if you was smart, you wouldn't start messing with another man's woman."

"I mess with your woman, Walker? I apologize."

There was laughter from the porch at that. Walker jerked an angry glance at the men up there, then swung back to Slocum. "You know who I mean. Miss Dory is Mr. Boldt's property. Don't nobody even lay an eye on Mr. Boldt's property when I'm around. That's my job."

"You ain't too good at it, then. I heard somebody snatched Boldt's bride for ransom. Where were you then, Matt? Or is your job only shooting off your mouth?"

Walker moved out into the dust of the street. "You take that gun off, and I'll show you what my job is."

The men across the way had moved down off the boardwalk, expectant grins on their faces. Several more had begun to drift up from down the block. Those from inside the hotel had all come out now and were crowded up against the porch rail. Slocum untied the thong binding his holster to his thigh, unbuckled the gun belt, and wrapped the belt ends around the holster. "Here," he said, and pitched it up to a man on the porch.

Walker was on him before he'd even turned around. The big man came on like a bull, head down, and butted Slocum in the side, his massive shoulders knocking Slocum down off the step. Slocum hit the ground and rolled, coming up on his feet to circle out of

Walker's reach, wanting time for his head to clear, to judge the man he was facing.

He sidestepped another bullheaded rush and hit Walker in the belly as he passed. That brought Walker's head up; he circled now, arms out, hands open—the man's style was to wrestle, which was all right with Slocum; one real blow from Walker's fist would likely lay him out.

Walker rushed him again, trying to get him in a bear hug; Slocum planted himself solid and hit the big man squarely in the nose. Walker grunted, his hands going to his face, where blood was gushing suddenly down his mouth. Slocum followed through with a hard left to the belly, which brought Walker's hands down but seemed to have no other effect on him at all.

The onlookers had come down into the street now. Slocum sensed rather than saw them crowding around him, forming a dense ring where he and Walker circled in the dust. He was dimly aware of encouraging shouts, catcalls, the sight of money clutched in several hands. Walker was shifting to his left, blood flowing unchecked from his nose. His little eyes looked angry. Slocum wondered if the man had ever been beaten; if not, a few more jolts like that bloody nose might enrage him enough to lose control.

Circling, he caught a glimpse of Dory watching from the hotel porch, eyes bright with excitement, breasts swelling above the low-cut gown. She called out something when she caught his eye, but he couldn't make it out above the shouting around him. And then Walker was coming at him again.

Walker drove him back against the tightly packed crowd this time; he felt the man's arms go around him, felt himself lifted up; then Walker slammed him to the ground like a man trying to break a slab of rock. He rolled to miss a kick from Walker's huge boot, came up in time to sidestep another rush, and hit Walker on the ear as hard as he could. Walker wheeled, and Slocum slammed his doubled fists around into the other ear.

Walker roared, reaching for him; Slocum grabbed a sleeve, felt it rip away in his hands, then Walker swung a roundhouse right that caught him on the cheekbone, then another on the jaw. He was driven back against the crowd, felt hands push him away, and then he was circling again, wary. Walker was stalking him now, the sleeve flapping from his bare arm, blood still coming from his nose. His ears had already begun to puff up. Slocum kept shifting to his left, staying beyond Walker's reach. He heard Dory shouting in his ear, saw she had worked her way to the front of the crowd, saw the marshal beyond her, watching from the boardwalk, shotgun cradled in his arms. He was vaguely aware that a wagon had pulled up just behind the crowd, two men watching from the wagon box.

Walker was closing on him, slower now, watching him with those little pig eyes, big hands out to trap him back against the ring of shouting men. Slocum knew he had to end this fast or Walker's superior strength was going to beat him. When he was almost out of room, with the crowd at his back, he feinted to his right. Walker shifted with him, and Slocum lunged back to his left. Caught in mid-stride, Walker took a wide step back to cut him off, and Slocum sent a vicious kick up into the big man's crotch.

A strangled cry came from Walker's throat. He bent to seize his crotch, and Slocum brought a knee up into his face, feeling blood spurt from the broken nose. Walker's head came up, and Slocum planted another kick square in the man's belly.

Walker went down, rolling in the dust, groaning, hands clasped between his legs. Slocum watched him warily, his own belly heaving to get enough air. The densely packed circle of men, unwilling to have their entertainment end so soon, was shouting at Walker to get up.

Dory moved out of the crowd, her face flushed with excitement, and prodded at Walker with one small foot. "Get up, Matt. Get up and fight. Do it for me, Matt."

Walker was just working his way to his knees when Slocum heard the rattle of the wagon and saw the men in the circle part to let it through.

The man holding the reins was small and slight and had the look of a gun hand. The other was around fifty, with a long, hook-nosed face that looked almost Indian, his black hair graying at the temples. He wore a wide-brimmed Stetson, with a brocade vest under a frock coat, and he had the air of a man used to wielding authority.

He dismounted from the wagon, tall and erect, and jerked his head toward the crowd. "Fight's over, boys. Go on back to your drinking. Matt, you're licked. Get up from there and go let the doc take a look at you."

He had an oddly hoarse voice, and a faintly humorous expression, as if he had seen too much of life to take a street fight very seriously. But there was a trace of steel there, too, that showed it wouldn't be smart to cross him.

Walker had got painfully to his feet and was wiping blood from his nose. "I ain't licked, Mr. Boldt. Let me take him. You don't know what he done. He—"

"That's enough," Boldt said. "You go on to the doctor. I'll take care of this now."

Walker mumbled something; he shouldered his way through what was left of the crowd, avoiding Slocum, and limped away down the boardwalk. Most of the crowd had dispersed, drifting back into the saloons. Only a few men lingered on the hotel porch, watching.

Boldt turned to the man still on the wagon seat. "Nolan, take the wagon on to the stable. Dory, I suggest you get in off the street." He turned those humorous eyes on Slocum, nodded once to the marshal, then took Dory's arm and led her back toward the hotel.

The marshal stepped down off the boardwalk, unlimbering his shotgun. "You just worked your way back into jail."

Slocum looked at him. "You put a man in jail for a fair fight?"

"One step out of line, I told you."

Slocum looked toward the hotel. The rest of the crowd had gone back inside. It was nearly dark now; light came from the windows along the street. The man he'd tossed his gun belt to was nowhere in sight. "You tell Sam Boldt I want to talk to him."

"Sam decides who he talks to and who he doesn't." Brady prodded him with the muzzle of the shotgun. "Now move."

Back at the jail, Brady shoved him into the same cell, locking the door with his ring of keys. "You're too late for supper, so I guess you'll just have to go without. Water bucket's under the dipper on this nail, right outside the cell here. You reach right, you can get yourself some water. Otherwise, just settle in."

"Tell Boldt what I said. There's something I want to talk over with him."

"From what I heard, there may be something he wants to talk over with you. Soon as he learns what that fight was about. You better give it some thought. Maybe you don't want to see him after all."

"I'll take the risk. Just tell him what I said."

"I'll do what I please," Brady said. "Be grateful you got a free bunk. You look like you could stand a rest." He slung the ring of keys on a nail over his desk and went out, leaving a lamp burning and the door open onto the street.

4

When Brady's footsteps had receded away down the boardwalk, Slocum sat up on the bunk and gingerly tested his rib cage with his fingertips. No ribs seemed broken, but he could tell he was bruised; he was going to be sore in the morning. There were several sore places along his arms, too, that he hadn't noticed before, and the pain in his knuckles was just beginning to make itself felt. Carefully he touched the raw place on his jaw and the bruise under his eye. The jaw had bled a little; it would scab over. The flesh on his cheekbone was puffed up, though, and painful to the touch.

He rolled up his sleeves and went to the bars and found the dipper on a nail just outside the cell. He dipped some water from the bucket and poured it over his head, rubbing his face, careful to avoid the sore spots. Then he ran a hand through his hair and went back to the bunk. *Well, Red,* he thought, *I hope you're worth it.*

Footsteps came along the walk an hour later, and the marshal came in, followed by the man who had been on the buckboard with Boldt. Brady took the ring of keys off the wall and came to unlock the cell door.

"Mr. Boldt wants to talk to you," he said. "Nolan here'll take you."

Slocum stepped out of the cell, rolling his shirt-sleeves down. "You letting me out for good, or am I supposed to come back here?"

"That's up to Mr. Boldt. You go on with Nolan. You been saying you wanted a talk. Now you got your chance."

Outside, Slocum felt a little naked without a gun on his hip. The man named Nolan showed no inclination to talk, just stayed close behind him, his boot heels ringing on the boardwalk. The town had livened up considerably since this afternoon; there were lights in every saloon he passed, and loud talk and laughter. He wondered if anybody had won money on the fight. Given Matt Walker's reputation in this town, the odds should have been long.

Boldt's place was humming when he swung through the bat-wing doors, the man called Nolan right behind him. Several men turned from the bar to survey him as he passed, and he heard the hum of conversation pick up as others around the room caught sight of him. Several faro games were going full-tilt at the tables in the other room, and music came from a melodeon near the back. He saw several fancy-dressed women working the crowd, but there was no sign of Dory.

Nolan guided him up the stairs and rapped on the first door along the hall. When the answer came, he opened the door for Slocum to step through and closed it behind him. Slocum found himself alone with Samuel Boldt.

Boldt sat behind a polished desk, facing the door, across a large high-ceilinged room with sofas and chairs arranged at either end of it. The windows on the left looked out on the street; on the right were a pair of closed doors that likely led into Boldt's private suite. And likely there was a man or two posted back there, ready to come in at the first sign of trouble.

Boldt was slicing off the end of a cigar with a penknife on a vest-pocket chain. He nodded toward a leather chair in front of his desk, slipped the knife back in his vest pocket, and put a match to the end of the cigar, turning it slowly between his fingers.

"I'm told you're an old friend of Dory's," he said, and glanced up over the match to see Slocum's reaction.

Slocum wasn't sure what the answer to that should be. Not even the worst of men could defend going to bed with another man's woman. And pleading ignorance of Dory's status would surely cut no ice. "Years ago," he said. "Back in Georgia."

"And Marshal Brady says you're looking for Red Wylie."

"That's right."

Satisfied with the coal glowing at the end of his cigar, Boldt flicked the match out and dropped it in a large ashtray. "You know where Wylie is?"

"Not exactly. I hear he's holed up somewhere in those canyons west of town. Brady said you might know where he is."

"There's several bunches hang around out in those canyons, living off what they can steal. I think Wylie is with Ashe Greene's bunch, the outfit that abducted Ramona Warren, my fiancée." He eyed Slocum over the cigar. "You have heard about that."

"I heard about it."

"They took her two days ago. She was out driving alone in a buggy, and she didn't come home. And that night somebody tossed a rock through my window, with a note tied around it. Said I had a week to come up with forty thousand dollars, or they'll kill her."

"Why tell me all this?"

"Because I want you to bring her back."

Slocum raised his eyebrows. "You want me to bring her back?"

"That's what I said. I was out there today trying to buy information on where Greene's bunch is holed up. Nobody was talking. They might not like each other out there, but they hold together against anybody that's not their kind. I figure a man like you, a friend of Wylie's, all you'd have to do is drop word you're looking for him, and he'll find you. That'd lead you to Ashe Greene."

"And you expect me to find where they got Ramona Warren and sneak her out without any of them seeing. Seems to me you're overlooking a couple of things.

One, I got no reason to try something like that, even assuming I'd take your side against Red. And two, your woman would get killed if I failed. Seems to me you're better off paying."

"I have no wish to risk Ramona's life," Boldt said. "But I didn't get where I am by taking no risks at all. I'll tell you what I have in mind. I want you to ride out there with the forty thousand in your saddlebags. If you can get her free without paying, I'll give you half of it. If it looks like you can't, you tell them you're representing me and pay the forty thousand."

"What makes you think I won't just keep on riding with it?"

Boldt smiled, the look of a man too sure of himself to take offense. "Because I'd have you tracked down and killed. And because if you did, Greene's bunch would kill Ramona, and I would trail every mother's son of them to the gates of hell to see them dead. Including the friend Dory tells me you rode all the way from Oregon to see put on the straight-and-narrow. But I'm gambling you'll want that twenty thousand. If you want to save your friend's neck, you'll go along with me."

Slocum thought about it. There was no good reason he shouldn't. He had done things as difficult in his life, starting with the war and that train he and Red had hijacked in Georgia back in '65. He wanted Red loose from that bunch, anyway; for $20,000, it was worth the extra risk to smuggle Boldt's woman free. He and Boldt shared that much: Taking no risks in life got a man nowhere at all.

"You sure you ain't making a mistake?" he said. "Matt Walker didn't seem to think I was on your side. Why should you?"

"Matt don't think. He reacts. And he didn't know the situation. It was the way you handled Matt that attracted my interest in the first place. Far as I know, Matt's never been beat in a hand-to-hand fight before."

Slocum noted how carefully they had skirted the

subject of Dory Baker. That told him he was in no trouble on that score. But maybe Dory Baker was. Maybe she didn't know it yet, but Dory Baker didn't mean as much to Sam Boldt as she thought she did. He figured that was her problem.

"All right," he said. "You got yourself a deal."

"Good." Boldt went into the room on the right and brought back a set of saddlebags, the flaps open to reveal packets of bills inside. "Forty thousand dollars." He closed the flaps and threw the saddlebags down on the desk. "You bring Ramona back here, with the money, and half of it's yours. I already told you what to expect if you don't."

"Ain't you forgetting something?"

"What's that?"

Slocum slapped his hip. "Something to protect all that money with."

"Ah, yes, I almost forgot." Boldt opened a desk drawer and brought out Slocum's gun belt, the belt ends still wrapped around the holster. "Remember, you've got only five days. If you can't get her free before then, you'll have to pay. That's the deadline."

"If I can't get her free before then, likely it can't be done." Slocum strapped on the gun belt and hoisted the saddlebags over his shoulder. "I'll have to find Red, and I'll have to find her and figure how to get her out, but I'll be back here within a week. Count on it."

The hallway looked empty when he left Boldt's office. He could hear music from downstairs, the hum of talk and the click of poker chips, but there was nobody in sight. He carried the saddlebags to his room and lit the lamp on the nightstand.

His war bag had been searched. Whoever had done it had put everything back, but not in the order he'd had it in. The bed had been pulled apart too; he could tell by the sloppy look of it. Undoubtedly one of Boldt's men, checking him out. Well, he hadn't had anything to hide, but he did now. These rooms couldn't be locked.

He dug out a length of rope he kept in the war bag for such emergencies and tied one end of it around the saddlebags, cinching the middle section in tight. Then he raised the window and looked out.

The moon was up, turning the landscape silver. The cattle down in the holding pens were quiet now, likely asleep on their feet. So far as he could tell, the back street was deserted. He could hang the bags outside and close the window on the rope, but they would be too conspicuous to anybody passing outside. He lowered them out the window, set them to swinging at the end of the rope and heaved them upward.

They cleared the eave and landed on the roof. He took the knife from the scabbard in his boot and reached up to cut the rope off even with the upper edge of the window, so it couldn't be seen from inside. Then he closed the window and left the room.

Downstairs, he ate his meal in silence, conscious of all the eyes on him. Somebody offered to buy him a drink, wanting to get him in conversation, but he waved the man off. One of Boldt's saloon women approached him, but he waved her off, too. There was no sign of Dory, nor of Matt Walker. He hoped the man had had to take to his bed.

Back upstairs, he checked to make sure the rope was still there, then stripped and got into bed. He slipped his Colt under the pillow, to put it within easy reach, and settled down to sleep.

5

He woke in the dead of night, sure that somebody was in the room.

Faint moonlight came from the window at his back, but he had risen out of dreams, his eyes still focused on blackness, and he couldn't see. Only some tiny tick in his ear, some sound he'd heard in his sleep, told him he was not alone. Without changing position in the bed, he snaked his Colt out from under the pillow and pointed it in the general direction of the door.

Then a hand touched the gun barrel, pushing it to the side, and he heard Dory's muffled giggle: "The right shape, and hard enough. But I had the real thing in mind."

His eyes began to adjust to the dark; he saw her bending over the bed, wearing a filmy black gown. The gown hung open down the front, and he could see she was naked underneath it, one pale strip of flesh visible in the moonlight: heavy breasts, the rise of her navel, the patch of blond curls where her thighs joined.

He slipped the Colt back under the pillow. "You're a little crazy, aren't you? With your Mr. Boldt just down the hall?"

"Crazy about some things. So are you." She crawled onto the bed beside him, letting the gown fall to her waist, bringing her elbows in to force her breasts together, so that they bulged out between her upper arms. She arched her back and looked down at herself. "Tell me you're not a little crazy about this."

"After you sicced Boldt's watchdog on me? I'd have to be crazy to want anything to do with you." But the

36

sight of her was already sending flashes of heat down into his belly, bringing him up and erect.

"I didn't sic him on you. Didn't even know he was around. And you want something to do with me." She raked the blankets down, giggled at the sight of him naked in the moonlight, and reached out to take him in her warm little hand. "This much of you does, anyway."

He started to seize her other arm, but her hand moved on him, slow and firm, palm pressure slowly descending and slowly rising again; and before he could protest, her head dipped down and he felt her mouth go around him, soft and hot and wet, felt it stroke down the length of him to meet her hand, and then back up again, and then down again.

Heat rose up the back of his neck; hot and blinding blood flooded his brain. He found her head with his hand, not even sure himself whether his intent was to stop her or to urge her on; and then her tongue slithered in a tight, wet curl around the tip of what she gripped in her hand, causing him to go weak with pleasure, and he forgot everything except the touch of those fingers, that mouth, that tongue.

He couldn't think, could only feel the soft wet embrace of her mouth, that agonizing rise and descent as her head moved, her hand gripping the base of him, stroking slowly up as her mouth moved up, slowly down as her mouth moved down again. Caught by surprise as he was, coming suddenly out of sleep to this, he felt himself near to losing control, and his hips rose up off the bed, his hands gripping the sheet, but she stayed with him, rising up with him, never altering that soft slow rhythmic stroking, denying him the hard and rapid lunging that something in him so desperately craved. Bucking, quivering, he arched up off the bed for what seemed the longest of minutes, tormented by that urgent desire for firmer contact; then, denied it, he fell back again, and she stayed with him even as he fell, her mouth never leaving him, that soft slow stroking uninterrupted—up, and down, and up, and down again.

He reached again to grab her head, wanting to hold her in place to give him something to lunge into, but she slipped her other hand down in between his thighs, five separate fingertips soft and delicate as feathers, and he felt his strength fade, and his hand fell away. For one long agonizing minute those soft fingers hovered and danced in delicate circles across his skin, then that hand crept up to close around him as well, so that now she gripped him in both hands, palm pressure tightening. He bucked up off the bed again, and for a moment he had what he wanted, that firm grip to lunge through, and he braced himself and drove up into her mouth, only the embrace of her hands barring passage into her throat. Lunging and lunging, almost gone now, he felt himself begin to lose consciousness, something like rapture rising up unwilled within him so that he was suddenly afraid he might cry out. And then her palm pressure slackened, her mouth stroked softly up to linger at the tip of him, her tongue began those slow circles, and again her head moved with him, rising when he lunged up, staying with him as his hips descended, and he fell back onto the bed, quivering and trembling, frustrated need raging through him.

Then her hands stroked firmly down to the base of him again and held there, pulling all skin taut, and he felt her thumbs slide up and begin to scrape at the hard flesh just below the embrace of her mouth, slow and calculated. He sensed her eyes on him, watching his reaction to the friction of her thumbs; her mouth sucked down till he could feel the sharp embrace of her teeth, her tongue moving in rapid circles, and he heard himself groan aloud, no longer able to contain it, his hands frantically searching for her. This time he succeeded in grasping her head, forcing her to stay in place while he plunged up into her mouth. He was loose now, plunging and plunging and plunging, fiercely gripping her skull; then he felt her neck stiffen, her elbows clamp down across his thighs, refusing to give in to the drive of his hips, forcing him into a restrained pace just below the speed he needed to take him over that peak he wanted so desperately to clear, and after what seemed an infinity of frustration he felt his strength leave him again, and he fell back, his hands dropping away to clutch at the sheet again.

After that he lost track. At lease twice more she did that trick, driving him wild until he was almost gone, then clamping down, denying him climax. By the time she finally let him go all the way, he was lost to consciousness, his eyes fiercely closed, his teeth clenched, his hips driving up in long slow plunges, held to that pace by the force of her hands and the weight of her upper body on his legs, so that the final release was even more powerful that if he had been free to thrash as rapidly as he wished—controlled and rhythmic and powerful, one long slow volcanic eruption that seemed to go on forever, till he collapsed exhausted on the bed to tremble and quiver under her hands.

She stayed with him even then, never letting him slip out of her mouth, delicate little hands slowly milking him; he felt her swallow, swallow again, and her lips caressed up the length of him and down again, sucking him into her, hard now, her tongue scraping across his suddenly sensitive flesh, sharp teeth raking slowly upward, bringing pleasure so intense it was close to pain, like bright lightning streaking down through the root of him into his groin, and he jerked away, pushing at her head, and this time he got free of her, gasping and twitching like a dying salmon.

She rose to her hands and knees, straddling him in the moonlight, eager eyes watching his face. "I learned a lot since Georgia," she said, and crawled up to kneel beside him, one warm little hand coming to rest on his chest. "I know things most men never heard of, things to drive a man wild."

He still hadn't caught his breath, but he could attest to that. There hadn't been many times he'd gotten so blown out of the world, been made so helpless by a woman's sexual skill, and he wasn't sure it was pleasant. Exciting, no doubt of that, so exciting you thought you'd go crazy, but not something he was sure he liked. Stay long enough around a woman who could do that to you, and you could end up losing your mind. Or your manhood, which was maybe the case with Red, who had been trotting along behind her for seventeen years, and her treating him like dirt all the time.

"It could have gone on," she said, something like glee barely contained in her voice. "You hadn't jerked away, it could have gone on, and that's when it really gets good. I've had men scream. I've had men groan and cry like you'd think they was being tortured, and after a while they ain't got strength enough to stop me. I done it three hours once to a man—he must have come six times, thrashing and crying out through the whole thing. Did it to him again the next morning, and when it was over he looked like I scared him to death." She laughed. "He steered clear of me after that, but you can believe he liked it while it was happening. But it takes a man can let himself go, let himself feel what he's feeling, and not many men can do that."

He still wasn't all the way back yet. He could feel the hazy heat slowly draining out of his brain, the hot blood seeping away from the surface of his skin, gradually receding down the back of his neck. His breathing was still the loudest thing in the room.

She slid a smooth hand across his middle. "Where's your fixings? I'll roll you a smoke."

"On the nightstand."

Still weak, barely able to move, he propped a pillow up behind him and dragged himself into a sitting position. Dory was shaking tobacco into a paper curled between her fingers; now she returned the sack of Golden Grain to the nightstand and set about rolling the cigarette. She was kneeling upright on the bed, pale moon-light shadowing all the hollows and swells of her body: the pink-nippled breasts, the curve of her belly, her sleek and slightly parted thighs.

"You talked to Sam, didn't you?" she said. "I seen Nolan bring you up."

"He got me out of jail, if that's what you mean. Where you got me put."

"I didn't put you there. Marshal Brady did." She licked the edge of the paper and crimped it down tight. "What did he talk to you about?"

"If he wanted you to know, likely he'd tell you."

She handed him the cigarette and struck a match from the box on the nightstand. "It was about Ramona, wasn't it?" She let the match burn on after the cigarette was lit, the flame's reflection dancing in her eyes as she watched his face. "He figures Red's part of that bunch that took her, and you being Red's friend could maybe get you in to where they got her hid. Ain't that right?"

"You got it figured out. What do you need me for?" He leaned up to blow the match out.

She raked a fingernail up his flank and laughed. "Need you for that. Ain't many men I've met can stir me up like you can."

He sucked smoke into his lungs and shaved the glowing coal in the ashtray on the nightstand. He was beginning to put this together—the sexual fireworks, the questions, the flattery. Dory Baker wanted something.

She was watching him, sitting upright on her knees, hands propped on her thighs, shoulders erect, creating a hollow curve at the small of her back and causing her rump and her breasts to thrust out like projections on a battlement. When she saw his eyes on her, she grinned and looked down at herself, elbows coming in to push her breasts out between her upper arms again.

"He's sending you out to pay that ransom, ain't he?"

"Why don't you ask him? You're his woman."

"He don't tell me nothing that has to do with Ramona. But I got ways of finding out. He's sending you out to pay the ransom, ain't he? Or to try to get her free without paying unless you have to.''

"What gives you that idea?''

"I saw you carrying those saddlebags out of his office. And I know how his mind works. Besides, like I said, I got my ways of finding out.''

"What do you care, anyway?''

"Because I can help you.'' She leaned suddenly down on her hands, big breasts swinging in front of his face. "I know where she is. I can help you get her loose. And then you and me, we can split that forty thousand and leave the country. You wouldn't have to pay it if I helped you.''

He took another drag, eyeing her speculatively in the faint glow from the coal at the cigarette's tip. "I thought you were Boldt's woman. You turning against him?''

"You know I'm on my way out. He maybe wanted me once, but he never asked me to marry him. She's got a deeper hold on him than I ever had, and before long she'll get him to dump me. And I'm past thirty. I'm too old to start at the bottom again. With half that money I could go somewhere and start my own place. I know how to put girls to work. I'd be the boss finally.''

"How is it you know where she is? And why ain't you told Boldt?''

"Why should I tell him how to get his new woman back? And the way I know is, Sam's right—it was Ashe Greene's bunch that took her, and Red's a part of it. Red still can't keep away from me. I always know what he's up to.'' She came down to snuggle up against him, breasts softening against his side, one shapely leg sliding over his. "What do you say, Johnny?''

"I'll sleep on it.''

He figured he didn't need her to lead him to Ashe Greene's bunch. He knew men like that, how they thought and what kind of place they'd pick to hide out in, how a stranger might make himself known without getting himself killed. He could find that hideout, and they wouldn't try to shoot him right off without some kind of parley. All he had to do was let them know he was a friend of Red's; they'd take him to see Red then, and he'd be home free.

Dory was fondling the hair on his chest, her head tucked down under his chin. "You know, Johnny, you ain't really known me since I was fifteen. I'm a woman now. You and me, we could split up that money and head for someplace like Denver or Chicago. We could have a good time together."

"And what's to keep Sam Boldt from tracking me down and having me killed?"

"You can take care of Sam. Or anybody he sent out to find us. I know you could." She came up on her hands again, leaning over him, and leaned down to kiss him, soft and lingering, her breasts brushing his chest. Then she raised her head and looked down at him, eyes examining his face. "Let's do it, Johnny."

"I said let me sleep on it." He stubbed the cigarette out in the ashtray. "I went through a beating today on account of you. The least you can do is let me get some sleep."

He tugged the pillow down into place, turned over on his side, his back to her, and settled down. He had no intention of taking her up on her offer, but she didn't have to know that yet. He could wake before her—years of sleeping out on hard ground had taught him to wake when he wanted—and by the time she discovered he was gone, he would be halfway out to those canyons. He'd seen bad news in Dory Baker even back in Georgia, when she was just fifteen, and what life had done to her since didn't make him trust her any more than he had then. And he had no reason to share that money with her.

It was not quite an hour later when he felt her stir in the bed. She had snuggled down behind him, warm against his back, one little hand resting on his ribs, and

for quite a while he had thought she was actually asleep.
He was sleepy himself, tired and sore from the fight
with Walker, but sleep wasn't something he could afford
with her in the room. For an hour he had forced himself
to lie still, holding his breathing regular, and though she
had seemed asleep, he wasn't surprised now to feel her
cautiously move away and rise to one elbow behind
him.

He sensed she was looking at him. "Johnny?" she
whispered.

He didn't move.

"Johnny, you awake?"

He didn't answer, didn't alter the rhythm of his
breathing.

After a minute or two, the mattress shifted as she got
out on the other side. He heard her tiptoe around the
bed, come up alongside him, stop. Even with his eyes
closed he could tell she was bending down to gaze into
his face.

"Johnny?" she said again.

He sensed her bending over him for a long minute,
watching his face. Finally he heard her move away, her
bare feet padding across the room, then small unidenti-
fiable sounds from near the door. He opened his eyes. It
was a moment or two before they adjusted to the moonlight coming in the window behind him. Then he saw
her kneeling on the floor, fumbling with his war bag.

She had it open, blindly searching through it. He
could see her identify an object with her hands, put it
down, pick up another. When she was satisfied neither
the saddlebags nor the money was in the war bag, she
closed it up again and sat back on her haunches, thinking. After a bit she glanced toward the bed, then went
to open the doors of the tall old chifforobe in the
corner.

Even in these circumstances she was a sight to behold,
that voluptuous little body naked in the moonlight, legs
made even more shapely by the way she rose on tiptoe

to feel along the chifforobe shelves, big breasts drawn up taut, round rump thrusting out below the arch of her back. Finding the chifforobe empty, she closed the doors and turned to survey the room, hands propped on her hips. He could imagine her lower lip coming out in that babyish pout he remembered she got when she was frustrated, and it made her look almost comic there, almost endearing.

She padded about to examine every corner of the room. Carefully, she searched the dresser, glancing toward the bed as she eased each drawer out and in. Then she turned to gaze at him, hands propped on her hips again, as if she might be able to read his mind. Finally she returned to the bed and ducked down to crawl up under it.

He found that close to comic too, picturing her worming about under the bed, naked belly and thighs inching across the cold boards, her breasts wiping up dust. He could hear her working her way from one corner of the bed to the other, hands patting blindly at the floor. Then she emerged out the other side, behind him, and got to her feet again. He heard her move to the window and carefully slide it up.

That brought him alert. He didn't dare turn around. Likely the rope was too small and too high up for her to see in the moonlight. And maybe too high to reach if she did. But she might know a way onto the roof, and that would complicate things considerably.

A long minute passed. Then another. Then he heard the window closing and she came back to the bed. She was silent for a moment, likely staring at him, angry that he had anticipated this and outsmarted her. He heard a frustrated little sniff, and then she eased back into bed.

So much for trusting Dory Baker. And maybe it wasn't smart to rely on waking before she did.

He waited another hour. By then he was sure she really was asleep, unless she was a better actress than he thought. This time he was the one who crept out of bed and slid the window open. It took him quite a while to tug the saddlebags down off the roof with as little noise as possible, but when he had them, he dressed as quietly as he could, retrieved his Colt, and picked up his war bag. He took one last look at Dory, then slipped out through the door and closed it behind him.

He rousted the hostler out of sleep—a different man from the one who had turned him in to Brady the day before—and by dawn he was a good two hours west of town, glad to have it behind him.

6

The road ran straight and dusty across the miles of prairie stretching away to either side. Except for a line of cottonwoods flanking an occasional shallow river, there was nothing but sagebrush from horizon to horizon. The day was going to be hot: An hour after it was up, the sun was already unpleasantly warm on the back of his neck.

By now Dory would have come awake to find him gone. That wasn't going to make her happy, and he didn't doubt that she could be treacherous when you got on her wrong side, but the price for staying on her right side was too high. And she and he had different things in mind. What had brought him here was his promise to old man Wylie to send Red home to Oregon, and with Dory around that would have been even harder than it was already going to be. Provided he could do it at all, in the midst of finding a way to get Ramona Warren free.

At about mid-morning he reined the gray down off the road under a little bridge crossing a dry riverbed and transferred the money from the saddlebags to a canvas sack in his war bag. Too many people knew about those saddlebags. Dory Baker knew, and the man called Nolan, and possibly Walker. No telling how many others. And no telling which of them might decide $40,000 was worth the risk of turning against Boldt. Dory thought so for sure, and if she had a man she could trust, that man had probably already set out after him.

At some point he was going to have to stash that money, but he figured to do that just before he was likely to encounter Greene's bunch. That way he could get at it quick if something looked to be going wrong. Now he left the empty saddlebags strapped on behind the saddle; anybody after the money would go for them first, and that would give him an edge. Not a very big edge, but maybe as much as he needed.

It was about two o'clock by the sun when he realized he was being followed. He had been easing his head around every now and then to check the road behind, but so far it was still clear. Now he saw a faint trail of dust off to the south of the road and about a mile back. Whoever it was seemed to be keeping pace with him. He eased around in the other direction and saw another trail of dust to the north of the road, about the same distance back, holding even with the first one. Two riders, trailing him out in the sage, thinking he'd consider himself safe if he saw a clear road behind him.

He watched them from the corner of his eye for half an hour before he decided they weren't after the money. Anybody after the money would have skirted around to get in front of him, to lay up in ambush somewhere ahead. He figured they were Boldt's men, set on his trail to see where he went. He should have known Boldt wasn't going to let him ride out completely alone, without somebody keeping an eye on him.

No telling what they had in mind, but whatever it was, it would be sure to foul things up. He didn't need any help, and maybe helping him was not what they were after. It had occurred to him before that Boldt could be using him as bait, a stalking horse to lead him to where Greene's bunch was. And bait was valuable only until it was used; you didn't care if it got chewed up when you made your catch. But they wouldn't do anything now, and there was no way he could lose them out here, with nothing but desert on either side. He would have to figure something out when he reached the shelter of the canyons.

The sun was just sinking toward the horizon when the

road took a turn into an ancient riverbed between the rock walls that marked the start of the canyon country. He had been watching the rocks coming up on the northwest horizon for some time; now he sent the gray into a trot, reining up just at the edge of the first bend, where he could look back across the prairie.

After a minute or two he saw the dust trails begin to angle toward each other, moving faster now. They would meet up on the road and stick together after that. And following the winding riverbed through the canyons would put him out of sight; they would have to come up closer behind him, just to keep from losing him. That would give him a chance. He turned the gray and kicked it on around the bend.

The road wound along between the rock bluffs for about another quarter mile. Then it came out onto open ground again, leaving the riverbed to stretch on west across the prairie. He followed the riverbed off to the northwest, where a hundred yards ahead it entered in between another set of cliffs, higher this time. It was only about thirty yards wide in most places and narrowed to less than ten in others, but at one time it must have been quite a river: He could see layer after layer of stratified rock high up the walls on either side, showing where the water had gradually eaten its way down. He had gone about a thousand yards when he found what he wanted.

It was a stunted mesquite tree growing out of a crevice in a narrow passage ahead. It looked to be about ten feet up the wall, growing out and up, and the trail bent out of sight to the right just beyond it. He didn't know how far back those two were, but he wasn't likely to find a better place. He slowed the gray to a walk as he came up toward the mesquite, stood in the saddle and reached up to grab the curve of the tree trunk. He let himself be dragged out of the saddle, kicking the horse in the rump as it passed beneath him, sending it on around the next bend at a fast trot. It wouldn't go

far, but he hoped there was no unsuspecting soul waiting around that bend, not with all that money stashed in
his war bag.

He got his elbows over the trunk where it bent to
grow up the cliff face, swung a boot around till he
found a foothold, and hauled himself up into the crevice. It was barely big enough to stand in, the crevice
walls extending out just far enough to conceal him, the
stunted tree providing cover in front. He drew his Colt,
braced himself against the rock, and waited.

Five minutes later he heard the plod of horses' hooves
coming at a walk along the riverbed. He figured they
would be single-file, approaching this narrow passage.
He eased his head out till he could see about twenty
yards back.

He saw the lead horse first, a black with a white
blaze down its nose, and then the rider—the man called
Nolan. Nolan passed directly below him, erect in the
saddle, head up, listening for sounds up ahead. He had
no gun out, but there was a Colt in his holster and a
Winchester thrusting out of the scabbard under the saddle cinch.

Nolan was barely past when the next rider came in
sight—Matt Walker, carrying a rifle, his face still showing bruises from the fight the night before. Slocum
would have preferred Walker in front—the big man
would be harder to take out this way—but he had no
choice.

He poised himself on the lip of the crevice, waiting
till Walker's splayfooted bay was directly below him.
Then he pushed away from the cliff face and dropped.

He hit Walker in the back with his doubled-up knees,
grabbing the man's collar and dragging him out of the
saddle as he fell. Walker hit the ground hard. Slocum
landed on top of him, clubbed him on the head with his
Colt, and threw himself behind the big man's bulk as
the bay reared and skittered sideways, squealing. Nolan
was fighting his horse around in the narrow trail up

ahead, his pistol out, trying to get the black around to get off a shot.

Walker was out cold; using the man's body for a shield, Slocum put a bullet over Nolan's head, the roar of the Colt echoing around the rock walls of the riverbed. "Throw your gun down," he shouted. "Throw it down. I got no reason to kill you."

Spooked, Walker's bay dashed across in front of him, blocking Nolan momentarily from sight, then skidded to a halt at the opposite wall and wheeled back to block him again. Nolan was still fighting the black, dodging for a clear shot, but the bay kept wheeling and dashing from one side of the riverbed to the other, frantic for a way out. Slocum leaped to catch it on its next pass, grabbing the saddle horn and letting himself be dragged along the sand. He heard the boom of Nolan's Colt, the whine of a bullet past his ear, then he snatched up the bay's reins and ducked to fire under its belly.

The black went down in a heap, shot through the lungs. Nolan was thrown clear, losing his pistol; he hit the ground and rolled, trying to get to the Winchester in his saddle scabbard, but Slocum put a bullet into the sand beside his head, and Nolan froze, his back to Slocum, his hands still outstretched.

"Hold it where you are," Slocum said. He had the reins in one hand, braced against the jerking of the bay, straining to keep the Colt trained on Nolan. He chanced a look at Walker—the man was still out. He fought the bay over toward Nolan, close enough so Nolan could hear the click of the hammer as he cocked the Colt again. "Back off," he said. "Don't get up, but back away from that horse."

Cautiously, Nolan got to his knees and edged back away from the dead horse, his hands above his head. Only when he was out of reach of the rifle in the scabbard did he turn to look at Slocum.

"You should have dropped that gun when I told you," Slocum said. "I don't like killing horses."

Nolan didn't say anything; he still had his hands raised, and he was watching Slocum warily, as if expecting a bullet in his head any second. Slocum found where Nolan's Colt lay half buried in the sand and kicked it farther out of reach.

"Now suppose you tell me why you been on my trail all day."

Nolan glanced at Walker, but the big man was still unconscious. "Why should I tell you anything?"

"Because you're a dead man if you don't. I want to know what you and Walker had in mind. You tell me that, and you can head back to your boss."

"Mr. Boldt wanted you trailed," Nolan said.

"And then what?"

Nolan eyed the Colt and licked his lips. "We was supposed to follow you to where Greene's bunch is. Find out where they got Miss Warren." He edged back on his knees a bit, glancing to where Walker still lay facedown.

"Come on. There's more."

"We was just going to report back then. That's all. Just report back."

"And maybe then Boldt was going to send some gun hands out here to raid the canyon, is that it? I'm risking my neck as it is. I don't want to get my throat slit for leading Boldt to Greene's hideout."

The bay had settled down. Keeping the Colt on Nolan, Slocum let go of the reins and moved to the black, sliding the Winchester out of the scabbard and slinging it a dozen yards up the riverbed. Then he crossed to retrieve the rifle Walker had dropped and did the same with it. The big man was still not wearing a handgun.

"Now you go back and tell Boldt I don't like being hoodwinked. If he wants me to do what I said I'd do, you tell him to keep away from these canyons. You, and Walker, and anybody else he might have in mind to send out here.''

Nolan was getting to his feet, still wary. "He ain't gonna like this.''

"That's your problem. Now get Walker up on that bay and get out of here. If there's any of Greene's bunch within earshot, that gunfire's probably got them headed this way. I want you gone before they get here.''

Nolan dragged Walker over to where the bay stood against the canyon wall. He hoisted the big man upright against the saddle fender, bent to grab him around the knees, and shoved him up over the horse's rump, head and arms dangling down the other side. "If he's hurt bad, if he dies, you're in trouble.''

"He's all right. He'll likely come to before you're halfway to town. Now get.''

Nolan mounted the bay and reined out away from the wall. "We'll meet again," he said. "Next time it'll be different.'' And he touched spurs to the bay's flanks and started back along the trail.

When the bay had disappeared around the bend, Slocum picked up Nolan's six-gun and stuck it in his belt. Then he holstered his own Colt and retrieved the two rifles. No sense letting good weapons lie out here to rust. The sun had just gone down, leaving a rim of fire on the farthest canyon bluff he could see. Shadows were already beginning to pool up along the walls of the riverbed. There was no sign of his horse, but it was rein-broke; it wouldn't have gone far. He bent to search through the saddlebags on the dead black, but they were empty. He was just straightening up, ready to whistle for his gray, when he heard a noise behind him, the sound of a shell being levered into the chamber of a rifle.

"Just ease those guns down on the ground," a voice said. "Take it real slow. Drop the rifles and your gun belt. Then you can turn around.''

He froze where he was, half bent over. He had picked the rifles back up after searching the saddlebags; now he had a gun in each hand and no way to defend himself. He put the rifles down, very carefully loosed his holster thong, unbuckled his gun belt, and let it drop around his feet, Nolan's Colt dropping with it to the sand.

Then he turned around.

7

There were two of them, both mounted, sitting their horses just at the edge of the next bend up the trail. The one on the left, a short square-built man wearing a poncho like a Mexican, was just bringing a Winchester down from his shoulder. And now Slocum saw that the other had the reins of his gray. However far it had run, they had found it; he hoped they hadn't had time yet to search his gear.

The man in the poncho was still holding the Winchester on him. "Looks like you had a little run-in," he said, nodding toward the dead horse in the sand.

Slocum held his hands out away from his sides, but he didn't raise them. He had no way of telling whether these two were part of Greene's bunch or of one of the other outfits that holed up in these canyons. Whichever they were, he needed them to think he was on their side, or at least not unfriendly; he had to give them cause to lead him to Red.

"Two of Sam Boldt's men followed me out of Bowie this morning. I kind of persuaded them to turn back. Had to shoot the horse out from under one of them, but they got the idea. That's my horse you got there."

"You mind telling why Sam Boldt would put two men on your trail?"

"I was asking around after a friend of mine. Red Wylie. Rumor in town is that Red's part of a bunch that snatched Boldt's woman for ransom. Likely Boldt thought I'd lead 'em to him."

The man in the poncho exchanged a glance with the

other. "Red Wylie, huh? How did you know where to
find him?"

"I didn't. I heard he was out in these canyons. I was
hoping I'd run into somebody that could direct me to
him."

"What do you want with Red Wylie?"

Slocum figured he'd been accommodating enough.
"That's my business."

The man studied him for a bit, as if trying to make up
his mind about something. Then he jerked his head
toward the gray. "Mount up. We'll go check out your
story. But I'm warning you, if you ain't what you say
you are, you may not live long."

They had already taken his Winchester—the scabbard
under the gray's saddle cinch was empty—but the war
bag and his bedroll were still strapped on over the
saddlebags. None of it looked to have been tampered
with, but there would be no chance now to stash that
money before he reached the hideout.

The second man dismounted to retrieve Slocum's gun
belt and sling it over the other's saddle horn. Then they
set out up the riverbed, the man in the poncho in the
lead, Slocum in the middle, with the other following
behind.

They wound along the high rock walls of the riverbed
for another mile or two, then cut up a rocky trail
heading vaguely north. After another mile of steady
climbing they came out onto a timbered bluff, and here
the trail gave way to sloping ground covered with pine
needles, leading up through the trees. A hundred yards
up the slope the ground dropped sharply off, the tips of
pines receding down a steep cliff face below them, and
near a large boulder at the edge of the bluff they picked
up the trail again, just where it started steeply down
through those pines.

The man in the poncho reined in beside the boulder
and waved Slocum up. "You first. And if you get an

itch to run, don't try it. That trail gets mighty narrow down below, and I'll be right behind you."

Slocum sent the gray down between the pines. After twenty yards he looked back. The man in the poncho was close behind him; he could see his gun belt swinging from the sorrel's saddle horn. The other man had dismounted by the boulder at the head of the trail and was rolling up a smoke. So that was where they kept a guard posted; wherever this trail led, it must be the only way in.

The trail got steeper a hundred yards down. Gradually the ground on either side changed, till the gray was picking its way down a narrow ledge, with a rock face rising nearly straight up on Slocum's left; the pines below got scrawnier and thinner till they, too, were gone, and he could see where they were headed.

The cliff was almost perpendicular now, and solid rock. The trail led straight down the south face of a perfect box canyon sheltered on all sides by high cliffs. The canyon looked to be about a mile long and a quarter-mile wide, and there was a strip of pines growing all around the bottom edges of it, where the grassy bottom sloped up to meet the cliffs. With the sun gone, twilight was creeping outward from the high bluff on the west, but he could see a double row of cabins about halfway up the canyon, four on a side, facing each other, leaving between them what had once passed for a rudimentary street.

It looked to be an abandoned mining camp. Through a break in the pines along the west wall, behind the last cabin on that side, he saw the black hole of a mine shaft, with a set of iron rails running down the slope from it. The rails seemed to peter out somewhere just to the north of that last cabin, between it and a little weathered corral. Likely ore had been carted out of that shaft and transferred to pack mules for the trip up this narrow trail. He could see another trail climbing the north face at the other end of the canyon, but that one looked even more treacherous than this one, narrower, and with stretches of it broken away by rock slides.

Twilight had set in for real when they reached the bottom of the cliff and cantered up toward the cabins. The first one on the left had lamplight showing in the windows, but the rest were dark. They reined up in front of the lighted cabin, a wide porch stretching across the front of it, and the man in the poncho glanced across at Slocum.

"You better be telling the truth," he said. "Either that or saying your prayers." He cupped his hands to his mouth: "Wylie? Wylie, you in there?"

Slocum saw a woman come to the window at the right of the door; she looked Mexican, young and black-haired. Two men drifted into view in the window on the left, and then another appeared in the doorway, slumped and tired-looking, with a worn gun belt sagging around his skinny hips.

"Yeah, Dooley," he said. "What's your problem?"

Dooley, the man in the poncho, gestured to Slocum. "Caught a man coming in through the canyons. Claims he's a friend of yours. You know him?"

It took Slocum a moment to realize that the man on the porch was Red Wylie. The hair was still red, but there was gray already eating into it at the temples. He looked worn and beat, like a man who'd seen too much of life and not found what he'd expected—more like his father, old man Wylie in Oregon, than like the youngster Slocum remembered from Georgia those long years ago. Red had been, what, then? twenty-one? twenty-two? That would make him maybe thirty-nine now, but he looked older, ten years older, wiry and thin, with his Adam's apple prominent in his stringy neck. He was looking up at Slocum with puzzlement on his face.

Slocum tipped back his hat. "You mean you don't remember me, Red?"

Red hesitated; then a tentative grin spread across his face. "Well, I'll be damned," he said. "John Slocum."

"You going to make me welcome, Red? So far I ain't had a real friendly reception."

"Well, come on down here." Red stepped off the porch, looking at Slocum as if he didn't yet believe what he was seeing. "Come on in and have a drink. My God, I never thought I'd see you again. How many years has it been?"

"You sure that's smart, Red?" Dooley said. "How well do you know this man? How do we know he ain't working for the law?"

"Know him? Hell, I've known him since I was green, since the war. This is Cap'n Slocum, my old commanding officer. And law? Hell, last time I seen him, we hijacked a train together. Here, give him back his gun." He took the gun belt hanging off Dooley's saddle horn, looking up at Slocum with something like wonder in his eyes. "Near twenty years, ain't it? My God, makes me feel how old I am."

"Well, I ain't got no younger myself, Red."

Slocum swung down out of the saddle, and Red took his hand, studying Slocum's face. "It's been a long time," he said. "Too long to think on, Cap'n. What in the wide world's brought you here."

"Looking for you, Red."

"You must have done some hunting to find me. Hell, we'll have to celebrate. Dooley, tell Maria to break open a fresh bottle."

"Tell her yourself." Dooley hadn't said anything while Slocum strapped his gun belt back on, but he didn't look happy with the situation. Now he dismounted and stalked into the cabin.

Slocum followed Red inside. It was just one big room, with a rock fireplace on the right, near a sideboard holding some pots and a dish or two. There was a door leading out onto a little porch in back, and a round table to the left of the door, scattered with glasses and playing cards, a half-empty bottle in the center of it.

The Mex woman was bending over a Dutch oven in the fireplace, stirring something cooking over the fire.

Dooley had poured himself a drink at the table; he downed it in one gulp, watching Slocum with wary eyes. The two men at the window had turned to eye him when he came in, and they didn't seem any friendlier. They both had the scruffy look of second-rate gun hands—one with a scraggly beard and a flat-topped hat with silver conchas around the rim of the crown, the other unremarkable except for a pair of shiny new boots contrasting oddly with the ragged and faded outfit he wore. Red made the introductions: The bearded man was called Fox; the one with the new boots, Runnion. He didn't bother introducing the woman.

"Dooley, you better get back up the trail," Red said. "You know Ashe wants two men on that bluff all the time."

"Let somebody else sit around up there," Dooley said. "Where's Quinn? It's about Quinn's turn."

"Quinn's standing . . . Quinn's busy. Fox, how about you going?"

The bearded man with the conchas on his hat was rolling up a smoke. "You don't give the orders around here, Wylie."

"Well, hell, you don't expect me to go. I ain't seen this man in seventeen years. We got a lot to catch up on. Dooley, Runnion—why don't you take a walk? Give a man some privacy."

Fox jammed his hat down on his head and went out. After a moment, Slocum heard a horse starting out toward the south bluff. Dooley and Runnion gave him a hard look, but they drifted out on the front porch and leaned against the porch rail, where they could keep an eye on the inside of the cabin.

"They don't seem too friendly," Slocum said.

"No, ain't nobody friends out here." Red slumped down in a chair at the table and poured a glass half full of whiskey. "You know a bad dog'll bite everybody but himself even if he runs in a pack. And these are all pretty bad. A man makes friends when he's young. After a certain age, you can hang around with a bunch, ride with 'em, drink with 'em, but they ain't really your friends. Least, that's been true with me. I ain't made a real friend since the war, since I left Georgia.'' He poured out a drink for Slocum and raised his glass. ''Here's to old friends.''

''How,'' Slocum said, and touched his glass to Red's.

Red drank off half the whiskey. The Mex woman was still at the fireplace, putting a lid on the Dutch oven; now she flicked Slocum a glance and went out the back door, disappearing down off the little porch.

''Who's she belong to?'' Slocum said.

''She's Ashe's woman. Shares the next cabin with him.''

''Ashe Greene? I heard in Bowie he ramrods the bunch you're with. Maybe I ought to meet him. He might not like a stranger riding in here. I get the feeling strangers ain't too welcome in these canyons.''

''Ashe ain't here. Besides, I'll vouch for you. Maybe you'll want to join up. That'd sure as hell please me. I don't know what Ashe would say. We got something— well, some of these boys might object to another chair at the dinner table. If you know what I mean.''

Slocum knew what he meant, and he knew what Red had barely avoided saying. They had something in the works, and the others wouldn't take too kindly to another man joining up just in time to get a share of the payoff. He figured he knew what the payoff was, too: the ransom for Ramona Warren. Which was right now sitting out there in his war bag, on the back of the gray. Just behind the rail Dooley and Runnion were leaning against.

Whatever pleasure Red had got from seeing an old friend hadn't lasted long. He looked a little melancholy now, as if the sight of Slocum reminded him of a younger self, when he'd had hope of better things. He had already finished his drink; he poured another and attempted a grin. "You still ain't told me what brought you here. I been hoping for years we'd run into each other, both of us drifting around out here. Daddy passed that last letter of yours on to me. I guess that was a couple years ago."

"Your daddy's who sent me. I was in Montana, thought I'd cut down into Oregon and look you up. Your daddy's ailing, Red. Thinks he's not got long to live. I kind of promised him I'd send you back. He wants you home before he's gone."

"Home," Red said. "Oregon never was home to me. And if he ever wanted me around, he sure had a funny way of showing it. He done drove me off last time. Said he never wanted to see hide nor hair of me again. So I took him at his word." He gazed off into the fireplace, where a low bed of coals was smoldering under the Dutch oven. "How bad is he?"

"He's bedridden. Nobody seems to know what it is. Just age, I guess."

Red brooded on that. Slocum had his eye on the porch, where he could hear a murmur of talk from Dooley and Runnion. He couldn't make it out, but every now and then one of them would glance his way. It was for sure they didn't like him being here. He had counted five men other than Red—the four he had met and somebody named Quinn. Busy, Red had said. Likely busy standing guard on whichever cabin they had Ramona Warren stashed in. Ashe Greene made six, and no telling how many others Greene had with him, or where they'd gone. He had to keep his back covered till he could find Boldt's woman and devise a way to get her free. He figured his best chance was to try joining up, like Red said. That wouldn't be easy. Red would back him, but Red clearly didn't rank too high around here.

"Red, about my maybe joining up here. Rumor in town says your bunch is the one that snatched Boldt's woman for ransom. Two of Boldt's men tried to trail me out here. I shook them off, but maybe you ought to tell me what I'd be getting into.''

Red's eyes darted nervously toward Slocum, then away again. ''We heard that rumor. That's all just talk. Once you're known as a canyon man around here, they'll pin anything on you. That's where Ashe is now—out checking to see who done it.'' The nervousness on his face told Slocum that was a lie. ''I don't say we don't run a crooked iron on a few stray cows now and then. Or even stop a stage out on the road. But we ain't taken no woman of Boldt's. Not that he ain't taken one of mine.''

''I know. I stayed at Boldt's place in Bowie. I ran into Dory there. You never did get over her, did you, Red?''

Red poured himself another drink. ''Well, you know, I told you about that once. Remember that letter I wrote you from Denver? Must be twelve, thirteen years ago now. I wrote that letter in a hotel room, drunk. Dory had just run off on me. First time. No, the second time, I guess—first time was in Oregon. Only then I thought it was just that she didn't like Oregon. When I caught up to her in Denver, I thought things'd be all right. And they was for a while. Anyway, that was the letter I told all that in. She'd run off about a week before, and I guess I stayed drunk the whole week. And come a Sunday, I think it was, nothing much happening, I sat there drinking all day in that room, looking out a window. Nothing lonelier than a empty street out a hotel window on a Sunday. And about dusk I rustled up a pen and ink from the desk clerk and wrote you that letter. Took me damn near all night. Don't you remember that letter?''

Slocum had never got any letter from Red in Denver. Likely Red had been too drunk to send it, or even to finish it. He looked to be starting on a fairly good drunk right now.

Red was staring into the fireplace. "You know what that reminds me of? Georgia. All that time ago. Funny how a thing fastens itself in your mind and keeps meaning something other than itself. I ain't been in Georgia, it's almost twenty years now. But every time I get like this, sitting around drinking, watching a fire in a fireplace, I think about Georgia. The old home place. Coon hunting. Dory sneaking out her window and creeping down that lean-to roof to go night-swimming." He glanced at Slocum. "Ever think about the war, Cap'n? I think about it all the time. And I ain't such a fool as to think it was as good as I remember it. I know things seem better when you're young. You got more life in you when you're young. But things *are* better then. Things taste better. They look better. I brung that up in more than one saloon when I had enough drinks in me, and everybody says it."

Slocum finished his drink and pushed the glass away. Red's problem was that he thought too much. One thing Slocum had learned was that it didn't pay to look back the way you had come. A man had to keep his eyes ahead of him or he might miss something important. A case in point being what he'd just seen—Dooley and Runnion leaving the porch and heading up to the cabin across the way. He saw a lamp flicker alight in the window over there; if he was going to scout around this place, now was the time to do it.

"When's Greene due back, Red?"

Red came out of his reverie. "Tomorrow. Said he'd be back about sunset. You want to talk to him about joining? I'd sure like it if you was to stay. I could get you to ride with me, I might even make it back to Oregon. One last time, anyway."

"I'll talk to him as soon as he gets back. All right if I turn my horse into that corral?"

"Well, yeah, I guess that's all right. I wouldn't wander around much out there. Like I said, these others ain't really friends. They wouldn't like a stranger snooping around. I'll save some of this bottle for you. You stable your horse and come back here, and then we'll find you a cabin to bed down in.''

He was still gazing at the fireplace when Slocum went out.

8

The moon was coming up over the canyon rim to the east. The night was warm, quiet; the silence always seemed immense when night fell out here in the desert. He paused in the shadows beside the door till he located Dooley and Runnion in the cabin across the way, sitting with their backs to the window, not watching him. Then he stepped down off the porch, untied the reins, and started leading the gray up the rutted stretch of ground between the cabins.

He had counted eight cabins when he rode in; of the four on his left, only two had lights showing—the one he'd just come out of and the next in line, the one the Mex woman shared with Greene. Except for the one Dooley and Runnion were in, all the cabins on the right were dark. That didn't mean anything. They had to be standing guard shifts around the clock, and there might be a man he hadn't met yet sleeping along here somewhere. And Ramona Warren, wherever they had her.

He had edged the gray to the right so that he was walking along the east row of cabins. Halfway up to the corral, he eased his head around to check the lighted windows behind him. When he was sure he wasn't being watched, he halted the horse and quickly untied one of the cords lashing his war bag on behind the saddle. He groped inside till he found the money sack and pulled it out. He had wanted to pick a better spot to hide it, but there was no chance of that now. He refastened the cord and started on, holding the canvas sack down close to his thigh.

He was coming up on the last cabin on his right.

When he got close enough, he pitched the sack up under the little porch in front, not breaking stride, not looking back. Then he angled the gray down to the left again, toward where he remembered seeing that corral. He hadn't seen a guard anywhere. That didn't mean anything, either. The man could be posted somewhere at the rear of one of the cabins.

He found the corral about fifty yards due north of the last cabin in the west row. A saddled horse was tethered outside the gate. There were four more inside, vague forms in the moonlight. He counted four saddles draped over the top rail, and four bridles hanging from a corral post. If he was lucky, if that Mex woman forked a regular saddle, there weren't any men he didn't know about. But where was the one named Quinn, the one he figured was guarding Ramona Warren?

He unsaddled the gray inside the corral and turned it loose. He hung the saddle over the top rail with the others and draped the empty saddlebags across it. He didn't like to leave himself afoot—he might want to get out of here in a hurry—but he couldn't afford to arouse any more suspicion than he already had.

He was just closing the gate when he saw a faint glow of light up behind the cabin directly south of the corral. It took a minute or two before he could make out what it was—the mouth of that mine shaft he'd seen on his way in, in the cliff face just up the slope from the cabins. He remembered there was a strip of pines along the bottom of the cliff, and a little break where those rails came out of the mine shaft. The glow was very dim, evidently coming from a light somewhere farther back in the shaft. That was why he had seen no guard on the cabins. They had Ramona Warren stashed in the mine.

Quinn would be in the shaft, then. Or posted just outside the opening. Slocum hoisted the war bag to his shoulder and started circling around the north end of the corral. He wanted to get a look at that mine shaft.

About forty yards of open ground lay between the corral and the first of the trees, a gentle slope reaching up toward the cliff. He climbed up through the trees, barely enough of them to provide cover, and turned left along the cliff face.

He drew his Colt when he reached the break in the pines. The mine shaft was another ten yards farther on, just beyond a little clump of scrub pine growing at the mouth of it. And now in the dim light coming from inside he could see Quinn, if that was who it was, sitting a few feet down the slope.

The man was hunkered down beside the rails running out of the mine, his back to the shaft. He looked to be whittling on a stick. Likely he felt pretty safe, hidden away in a box canyon, with two guards posted on the trail in, and this whole canyon country populated by badmen who would show no welcome to the law. But even a man who felt safe had ears. Carefully putting one foot in front of the other, Slocum starting easing along the cliff face toward that clump of pine.

He was almost to the mouth of the shaft when his boot dislodged a small rock, sending it skittering down alongside the rails. He ducked down behind the pine clump, bringing the war bag around in front of him, hoping it would blend with the branches.

Quinn turned and got to his feet, looking up the cliff face. Likely he thought it was a pebble that had worked itself loose from up there; rocks were always doing that on a steep bluff. Slocum held his breath as the man took a step or two up the slope to look into the mine. In the dim light coming from within, he could see Quinn was younger than the others, in his twenties, with sandy hair growing down past his ears. Satisfied, the man returned to his hunkered-down position and took up his whittling again, his back once more to the mine shaft.

Slocum waited five minutes, letting Quinn settle down. Then he rose carefully and quietly from behind the little clump of pine and eased around the corner into the mouth of the shaft.

Ten feet into the mine, he flattened himself against the wall on the left. Sitting down the slope as he was, Quinn was out of sight. The shaft ran level here, and straight back for about thirty feet, then took a bend to the left. The light was coming from somewhere just around that bend. If his count was right, there wouldn't be a second guard back there, but there was no sense taking chances. Keeping his Colt ready in one hand, carrying the war bag in the other, he started slowly along the wall, avoiding the rails in the middle of the shaft.

He halted just where the bend started around to the left. The light was brighter here. Four small kegs stood up against the opposite wall, a dull greenish color, like old copper. Black powder—miners kept black powder in copper kegs. He set the war bag down and eased his head around the bend.

The shaft widened into a small chamber here. Three wooden storage chests lined the wall on the left. The light was coming from a kerosene lantern on the one in the middle. A water bucket with a dipper in it was sitting next to the candle. And huddled up against the first chest was the girl.

She had her back to him, her head lying on her arms cradled on top of the chest, her face obscured by her long red hair. She wore no jacket, only a tight-waisted dress with a high collar and a full skirt. Even with her knees tucked up under her he could tell she was tall and slim and long-legged. And now he saw why they hadn't bothered to tie her hands—there was a shackle on her left ankle, connected to a chain wound around the near rail.

The rails disappeared into the dark of the shaft where it began to descend beyond the chamber. The wooden chests looked to be left over from the operation of the mine, and they were too small for anybody to hide behind. When he was sure she was alone, he holstered his Colt and slipped around the corner into the light.

She heard him just before he reached her. Her head came up off her arms and she turned, startled, a flicker of fright passing across her face. He knelt down beside her and put a finger to his lips.

"It's all right. Sam Boldt sent me out here to get you loose. The name's John Slocum."

He could see why Boldt preferred her to Dory. She was a good deal younger, maybe twenty-three or twenty-four, and it would be no exaggeration to call her beautiful. Set against a tumult of wild red hair, her skin looked as white as milk. Her mouth was wide and full, and now that she had turned, he saw the way her breasts thrust the bodice of her dress out, large and heavy above her slim waist.

She was studying him with big, green, intelligent eyes. "I don't understand. How did you get in here? Where are the others?"

"*Shhh*. There's still a guard out there. I sneaked in past him. One of this bunch is a friend of mine. They think I'm just here to see him, maybe join up."

"You're to get me free? But how?"

"Don't know yet. Your friend Boldt sent the ransom out with me, but he wants me to get you loose without paying it if I can."

"You have the ransom, but he doesn't want you to pay it?"

"Not unless I have to."

She looked away, as if to shield the anger on her face. He didn't blame her; it couldn't be pleasant to learn the man you were going to marry valued money more than he did you.

"They keep you in here all the time?" he said.

"They have so far. The Mexican woman brings me meals, but she always has a man with her. They had a guard in here watching me that first day, but they've left me alone since then. There's nothing I can do, anyway, shackled like this."

"How many are there, do you know?"

"I can't say for sure. Four or five of them stopped the buggy, but they blindfolded me right away. There's usually a different man with the woman every time she comes in, but I don't remember how many."

A sudden sound brought his head around, but it was a bat wheeling across the entrance to the shaft. "I got to go now. But don't worry, we'll find a way out of here. Worst comes to worst, I'll pay that ransom."

He left her then and eased back around the bend to retrieve his war bag, flattening himself against the wall and drawing his Colt again. This might be harder, coming out with the light behind him. He started edging along the wall toward the mouth of the mine.

Quinn was still sitting beside the rails down the slope, but he had stopped his whittling. His arms were crossed over his upraised knees, his head slumped forward. Bored, most likely. Slocum slipped out of the shaft and made his way along the cliff wall till he reached the shelter of the pines on the right. Then he holstered his Colt, shouldered the war bag, and started down toward the cabins.

So far he hadn't the slightest idea how he was going to get her out. He hadn't counted on them using a shackle and a chain; that would be hard to get off. And that itself might turn out to be the easiest part. The best bet might be to work on Red. There wasn't any love lost between Red and his mates in this bunch; if he saw he could trust Red enough to tell the truth about why he was here and offer to split that $20,000 with him, he might be able to get Red to throw in and help him.

He was passing along behind the west row of cabins now, little roofed-over porches, only about a yard square, tacked onto the backs of them. He saw the Mex woman in the cabin she shared with Greene, then he halted behind the first one, where he had left Red, bracing himself. When he had his wits about him, he mounted the porch and stepped inside.

Leaning against the wall across the room, just inside the front door, was Dory Baker.

9

His mind went suddenly blank. For the first time he felt the lack of sleep from the night before: He was too slow to react. Red was sitting at the table, glaring at him. And now he sensed somebody beside him—Dooley and Runnion, one on either side of the door, both of them pointing six-guns at him.

"Drop the war bag and raise your hands," Dooley said.

Dory was still leaning back against the wall, arms folded, watching him, a faint trace of anger on her face. Anger and a kind of amused triumph, pleasure at the revenge she was getting for his having left her as he had. He had no doubts about why she was here. And with two guns trained on him, it was senseless to resist. He dropped the war bag and raised his hands.

"You mind telling me what this is all about, Red?"

"Dory says you're working for Boldt. Says Boldt sent you out here to rescue that woman of his."

"Thought you didn't have her, Red. Why would I come out here to rescue a woman you don't have?"

Dooley had stepped over to lift the Colt out of Slocum's holster. "Let's cut the shit," he said. "You know we got her. We know why you're here. Bluffing won't work."

Now Red drew his own Colt, but he just laid it on the table in front of him, as if still not wanting to believe he needed it. "Where's the money, Cap'n?"

"What money is that, Red?"

"Dory says Boldt sent you out here with the ransom."

"And you believe her?"

"That's forty thousand dollars, Cap'n. It's for sure I don't want to think you'd work against me, but you and me, we ain't seen each other in seventeen years. And Dory's got no reason to lie. Now where's the money?"

"I ain't got it, Red."

"He's got it," Dory said. "Sam gave it to him in a set of saddlebags. Check his horse, Red. He's got it."

"Dooley, did Slocum have saddlebags on that horse when you brought him in?"

"Yeah," Dooley said. "Yeah, he did. Saddlebags, a bedroll, and that war bag there."

"Go up to the corral and bring the saddlebags down here. Bring the bedroll, too. We'll see who's in the right about this. Cap'n, just stand back against that wall. Unbuckle your gun belt and let it drop. You keep an eye on him, Runnion. Dory, bring me his war bag."

Slocum did as he was told. Dory crossed the room, casting a sidelong glance at Slocum, and dragged the war bag over to Red. Red hoisted it onto the table, opened it up, and began pulling out everything inside—Slocum's extra handgun, an extra bridle, a length of rope, a spare set of clothes. Slocum had his back to the wall, his hands still raised, watching. With Dooley out of the room, this might be the best chance he would get to make a break for it. From the corner of his eye, he could see Dooley's horse still tied to the hitching rail outside. But even if he could get to it without getting killed, there was nowhere to go. Fox and that other man were still posted on the south bluff; breaking out would cause such a hullabaloo they'd be alerted long before he got there. There was that little trail he'd seen up the north wall as he'd come in, but it had looked barely passable. Likely a man would have to cross several rock slides afoot, leading his horse, and he would never make it with this bunch hot on his heels. As things stood now, he wouldn't make it as far as the porch.

Runnion had placed himself beside the door, his gun still trained on Slocum's belly. Red was busy dragging out the last of the stuff from the war bag, but Dory had picked up his Colt; she held it idly in her hand, but her finger was on the trigger, and she was watching Slocum with a pleased little grin just turning up the corners of her mouth.

Dooley came back in, carrying the bedroll draped over his shoulder. He threw the saddlebags down on the floor. "Saddlebags are empty."

"No money in the war bag, either," Red said. "Open up that bedroll."

While Dooley untied the things around the bedroll and laid it out on the floor, Red retrieved his Colt from Dory, eyeing Slocum as if to learn some truth from his reaction. Dooley stripped the bedroll apart, patted the corners of it, and felt along all the seams.

"Nothing."

Red holstered his Colt. "Maybe you're wrong, Dory."

"I'm not wrong," she said. "Haven't I been right about everything else? From the very beginning? Sam told him he could have half the money if he could get Ramona free without paying. He must have stashed it somewhere on the way out here."

"Is that true, Cap'n? Boldt promised you half that money?"

"You believe what you want to believe, Red."

"I don't know what to believe. I don't like to think an old friend's turned against me. Not if it can't be proved."

"Old friends will do a lot for twenty thousand dollars," Dooley said. "Dory ain't never been wrong before. Why should she be wrong now?"

Dory had picked the saddlebags up off the floor; now she threw them on the table in front of Red. "Red, I should think by now you'd believe me when I tell you something. Take a look at the initials on that flap."

Red turned the saddlebags around to get a look where Dory was pointing. Slocum couldn't see the flap, but he could tell what was there by the expression on Red's face.

"S.B.," Dory said. "Sam's got his initials on everything he owns. And those are the saddlebags he gave Slocum the money in."

Red stared at the saddlebags for a moment; then he pushed them away and slumped back down in his chair. "So you are working for Boldt. Looking to sell me out. Where's the money, Cap'n?"

"I can't tell you, Red."

Red flushed and looked away. "Dooley, take him up there and put him with the girl. Put a double guard on them."

"I say we ought to beat it out of him," Dooley said.

"He's still a friend of mine. Give him time to think about it. At least till Ashe gets back. Put him in the mine and chain him to the girl."

"Better not," Dory said. "Slocum's smart, Red. You know that. Put them together and he may find a way to get them both loose. Put him in one of the cabins. And you'd better tie him up, too."

"All right. Put him in the cabin below the mine. That way whoever's guarding the girl can keep an eye on the cabin, too. And tie him to the bunk."

For a moment Slocum considered making a run for the door—but he would only get himself killed. He let himself be wrestled around while Dooley started tying his wrists together behind his back.

So far it looked like Red could hold these others off till Greene got back. He could maybe find some way to get loose before then, maybe overpower whatever guard they put on him. If he could get out before dawn, he might catch the rest of them asleep. He could get to that money then, and maybe to the girl, and then he could try that trail up the cliff at the north end of the canyon. It was worth holding out for a while, anyway.

Dooley finished tying his wrists and shoved him toward the back door.

"Look in his boot for a knife," Red said. "Slocum always carried a knife in his boot."

"And make sure you tie him to the bunk," Dory said.

Dooley found the knife and tossed it onto the floor beside the bedroll. "Don't worry, he ain't getting loose. Come on, Runnion."

They herded him up the path behind the cabins till they reached the last one in the row, directly below the mine. Quinn was indistinct in the dark, but Slocum could still see the faint glow coming from inside the shaft; it was just as well Ramona Warren didn't know what was going on down here. Runnion rattled the door open; Dooley prodded him up onto the little porch and inside.

The windows were boarded over; it was as dark inside as the bottom of a well. He heard Runnion's footsteps shifting uneasily ahead of him, searching for the bunk. "Over here," Runnion said, and Dooley prodded him again, pushing him forward. His knee encountered something hard—the edge of the bunk—and then he felt a hand in his back, a shove, and he fell onto a thin hard mattress.

"Not so tough now," Dooley said.

He heard their breathing in the dark; his feet were seized, pulled toward the foot of the bunk. A rope went around his ankles, and he felt it snugged down tight.

"Let's see you get out of that," Dooley said, and then the two of them were gone, the door slamming shut behind them.

10

The mattress was just a large sack filled with corn shucks. It was very old, the corn shucks worn down to no more than an inch or two thick. He could tell there was a solid slab of wood beneath it. No springs, and springs would have been useful—he could maybe have worked his hands down to bend a spring up and saw the rope in two on it. But these were crudely built cabins and makeshift bunks; there had to be something—a splintered board, a loose nail. If need be, he could swing himself down off the bunk by his feet and hunt for a nail head somewhere within reach on the floor.

Now that his eyes were growing used to the dark, he could see more than he'd thought. He was facing the back door; he could see moonlight around the edges of it. And the mortar had crumbled away here and there between the logs of the walls, letting in more moonlight. Awkwardly, he twisted his head around till he could see behind him. As far as he could tell there was no more furniture in the cabin. He saw the dim outlines of a big rock fireplace in the wall behind the head of the bunk, but that was all.

He heard somebody moving on the back porch, and he brought his head around. Silence now, but there was somebody back there. Likely Dooley or Runnion, or maybe somebody else he hadn't met—he still wasn't sure how many of them there were. So whatever he did would have to be quiet. He edged over till his hands found the bunk frame under the mattress—wood, felt like a two-by-four. He began feeling along it with his fingers, looking for a nail.

He hadn't looked long when he was brought alert by the sound of voices outside, boots scraping on the back porch. He recognized Dooley's voice, and Red's—too low to make out, but it sounded like they were arguing. Light quivered through the cracks around the door: a lantern swinging in somebody's hand. The voices came closer; he heard Dooley say something, and then Red's angry reply: "I said I want to talk to him alone. You think I'm trying to sneak him out? There's only two doors on this thing, and you got a man on both of them. Just stand aside. I'll be out in a minute."

He heard Dooley say something else, and then Red again, quieter now but sullen. Whatever it was worked; above the murmured talk came the rattle of the latch. Red stepped inside and closed the door behind him.

He was carrying a lantern, but the Colt was missing from his holster. That was evidently the price he'd had to pay to convince Dooley. The lantern light cast eerie shadows up across his face, but even so Slocum could see he was edgy, half angry and maybe half ashamed, caught in an awkward situation.

"I'm sorry, Cap'n. Don't like to see you this way. But you know I had no choice." He came over to sit on the edge of the bunk and snaked a cigarette from his shirt pocket, already rolled. "Brought you a smoke."

Slocum shook his head. "No, thanks, Red."

Red looked at him, studying him, as if not wanting to hear what he'd heard. Reluctantly, he returned the cigarette to his pocket. "I don't understand this, Cap'n. You can't get out of here. You don't talk before Ashe gets back, those boys out there'll get pretty rough on you."

"And you'll let them?"

Red looked down, sheepish. "I ain't got much say in this outfit, Cap'n. Had a little just now 'cause you're a friend of mine. Otherwise I ain't got much. And sure none when Ashe is here."

"Or when Dory's here."

Red was silent for a breath or two, likely letting that one sink in, maybe wondering whether to take offense. Then he shrugged. "Why you want to hold out on me like this, Cap'n? It ain't like Boldt was a friend of yours. Or Ramona Warren. Why hold out now, when it's me? And when you stand a chance of getting stomped, maybe killed?"

Slocum wondered what to tell him. It was for sure he didn't plan on getting killed. But Ashe Greene wouldn't be back till late tomorrow afternoon. There might still be a chance even if he didn't get loose tonight. They would have to bring him food and untie him so he could eat it. They would have to take him out once or twice, if only to let him take a leak. He could maybe trick a guard and get himself a gun. But he couldn't tell that to Red. And if he gave in, he would lose any leverage to talk Red into going back to Oregon. Once he had his share of the money, Red would be flush, too high-spirited to listen. That wouldn't be good. Red was clearly on a down slide; he didn't have enough pride left to keep from being ruled by a woman with a cruel streak in her, or by a two-bit badman like Dooley. A man without pride didn't last long among men like these. Another year or two of this life, and Red would get himself killed. Either shot in some squalid argument, or hanged at the end of a rope.

"I gave my word, Red."

"To Boldt? Hell, it don't mean nothing to give your word to Boldt. He ain't exactly a saint, either."

"When I give my word, Red, it means something. Who I gave it to is not the point."

Red reached down to fiddle with the lantern, as if needing something to do with his hands. "Well, it's been a long time since we known each other well, Cap'n. Likely life's been different to us. I don't know if we think the same way anymore."

He looked a little pensive, withdrawn, like maybe those memories of Georgia and the war were coming back into his mind. Likely it shamed him to have Slocum see how little standing he had in this bunch, how little even he thought of himself. The young Red that Slocum remembered, cheery and energetic, would never have bad-mouthed himself like Red had just done.

"I guess Dory gave you quite a run for your money, didn't she?" Slocum said.

Red gave him a sharp look. "Don't talk against Dory to me, Cap'n. She's maybe give me some hard times, but we had some good times, too. And you give up all claim to her back in Georgia. Seventeen years ago."

"I don't want any claim to her, Red. I just don't like to see what she done to you."

"Anything got done to me, I done it myself." Red went back to fiddling with the lantern, clicking the lever that brought the glass up from around the wick. "Been awhile since I could say she was mine, anyway. She's always taken up with somebody here and there. Some man with money and power. Boldt's only the latest one." He flushed, as a new thought came: "Right now she's having a thing with Sandy Quinn. He's standing guard out there on the slope right now. And sure, it hurts to watch it. He's young, better-looking than I am. But she'll tire of him. She always does. And she'll come back to me when she's down. Ain't nobody else cares about her the way I do."

"Don't look like she cares about you much."

"She cares. In her way, she cares. I been sticking to her for seventeen years. She knows she can count on me. And long as I know she'll come back when she needs me, that's enough."

"You're a fool, Red."

Red glanced at him, angry. "Harsh words, Cap'n. I wouldn't take that off just anybody. And I could maybe say the same about you. Tied up in here, surrounded by men that would as soon kill you as look at you. When all you have to do is tell where the money is."

"You guarantee that, Red? I go free if I talk?"

That little flash of shame passed across Red's face again. "I maybe couldn't, but Dory could. She set this thing up. You maybe guessed that by now. She don't control Ashe, but he listens to her. Those boys out there wouldn't let you go, but she could get Ashe to do it. You and the girl. All you got to do is hand over the money."

"I think Dory's got more power in your mind, Red, than she's got for real. I doubt if Ashe Greene ever aimed to let Ramona Warren go. Right now it's only rumor that it's his bunch that did this. Nobody can prove it. But Ramona Warren could. Put her up in front of a judge, she could hang the whole bunch of you."

"So could you."

"That's what I mean, Red."

Red seemed to let that sink in. Then: "We get that money, we'll be long gone from here. Won't nobody be able to find us, much less hang us."

"Not if Ramona Warren gets killed. I talked to Boldt, Red. Don't forget that. He said he'd track every mother's son of you to the gates of hell. That's the way he put it. And, sure, Dory's right—I told him I'd get his woman out of here for half that money. These ain't your friends, Red. Throw in with me. Help me get out of here, and I'll split my half with you. You and me, we'll go back to Oregon. That much money'd buy you a good-sized chunk of land in Oregon."

"Now you're asking me to go back on my word, Cap'n. Turn against my partners. I can't do that."

"They'd turn against you in a minute."

"Maybe. That don't matter. I guess you and me are alike that way. Raised the way we was, in the Old South—a man don't turn against his partners."

"Well, Red, I guess that kind of leaves us in a Mexican standoff."

Red gazed off across the room, as if unwilling to admit it. "Yeah. Yeah, I guess it does." He turned back to Slocum. "I hate to see it come to this, Cap'n. You and me on different sides."

"Well, Red, a lot changes in seventeen years."

"Yeah. Yeah, it does." Red stood up and picked up the lantern. "I figure you're fooling yourself, anyway. I wouldn't trust Sam Boldt to hand over twenty thousand dollars. I'll try to get Dory to talk to Ashe, Cap'n, but if you don't tell where the money is, I can't promise you'll leave this canyon alive."

When he was gone, the door closed behind him and the cabin dark again, Slocum watched the lantern's light quiver and quaver away through the little chinks between the logs. He could tell from the sounds that there was still a man on the back porch, likely still Dooley—and likely one on the front porch, too. He knew he ought to be hunting for a nail, or a split in the bunk frame, anything to saw that rope against, but the lack of sleep was beginning to catch up to him; he had that hot hazy feeling in his head and the ache around his eyes that came when he'd been awake too long. The talk with Red hadn't helped; he didn't like to think about what life had done to Red. He didn't want to think about anything but sleep. And if that meant there would be no escaping this cabin tonight, well, a man often thought he could do things he couldn't. After a while, nature took over and taught you you weren't as strong as you'd thought.

11

He was working on a nail in the bunk frame the next afternoon when he heard Dory's voice coming through the back door.

He had been awake about three hours. He had hoped to wake at dawn, but the long stretch without rest had kept him asleep till long after noon. Shortly after he woke, the door had opened and Fox, the bearded man with the conchas around the crown of his hat, had looked in on him; a short time later the Mex woman had brought him something to eat. They had untied his hands for that, but the door was left open and Fox had lounged on the little porch in back, a shotgun cradled in his arms, watching. When he'd finished eating, they had taken him out to relieve himself, but they hadn't left him alone even then—both Fox and Dooley had stayed with him that time, and both of them had had shotguns. Back in the cabin, his wrists bound behind him again, his ankles retied to the foot of the bunk, he had set about finding some way to saw that rope in two. He had taken a good look at the fireplace in the wall behind the head of the bunk; it looked big enough to allow a man to crawl up the chimney. He would worry about what to do then when the time came.

It hadn't taken him long to find the nail, just inside the bunk frame on the side away from the back door. He had to shift to the edge of the bed to reach it, arching back and working his hands in under the mattress. The nail had been driven up through the bottom plank and hammered flat into the wood of the two-by-four that connected to the bedposts. He could just get a fingernail under the tip of it, and he had been picking at it for the better part of two hours now, gradually working it out away from the wood. He had just got it to where he figured he could try cutting the strands of the rope when he heard Dory talking to somebody outside.

He could tell by the light that the sun was already low in the sky. Ashe Greene was due back about sunset. The last thing he needed was Dory coming in here to talk him loose from that ransom. But he heard the rattle of the latch, and Dory stepped inside.

Whoever was standing guard closed the door behind her. She was wearing a short, embroidered vest over a black silk blouse and a full skirt that buttoned down the side all the way to her ankles. Little black riding boots peeked out from beneath the skirt, and the vest was held across her breasts by a single leather lace. In the soft light filtering into the room, he saw a mix of emotions pass across her face: concern; apprehension; that strongwilled determination that had brought her all the way from the backwoods of Georgia. And under it all a kind of pleased amusement at seeing him brought low.

"Did you sleep well, Johnny?"

"Well as can be expected. What do you want?"

"I want to talk to you." She crossed to the bunk and crawled up to kneel beside him, the skirt making a valley between her thighs. "Ashe'll be back soon. Don't you think you ought to tell where the money is before then?"

He saw she had taken special care with her looks. There was a hint of rouge on the childish pout of her mouth, and her lashes were darkened to set off her eyes. He had to admit she was lovely to look at, that black blouse making her skin look as blond as her hair, the sleeves puffed out above her delicate little hands.

"I don't want to see you hurt, Johnny. You tell me where that money is, and I can get you out of here. Before Ashe gets back. If we worked it right, the both of us could get out of here. We could have the whole forty thousand to ourselves."

"You didn't seem to mind me getting hurt when I was fighting Matt Walker. I remember you trying to get him up so he could come at me again."

She shrugged. "I guess I was mad at you. Still am, a little. Have been ever since you told me no in Georgia. I'd have gone away with you then, if you hadn't said no. But we could work that out." She laid one little hand on his leg. "I'm not fifteen anymore. You and me could have a pretty good life together. But not unless you tell me where the money is before Ashe gets back."

"If I wouldn't tell Red, why should I tell you?"

"Lots of reasons." She undid the lace holding the vest together; when the sides of it parted, he saw the full swell of her breasts under the blouse, the buds of her nipples pushing out the cloth; she wasn't wearing anything underneath it. She ran her hands up across her breasts and started unbuttoning the blouse at the neck. "I'll show you a reason. You can't say being with me's not special. I know it is. I've known a lot of women in my business, well enough to learn what they're like in bed. And I know I'm special. So do you. You could feel it even back in Georgia, when I was just fifteen."

Her fingers had been steadily unbuttoning the blouse as she talked; now she loosed the last button and pulled the blouse open, shrugging it down over her shoulders. Her breasts spilled out; back arched, thighs spread, she cupped them in her palms, watching the expression on his face. "You don't even know yet how good it can get with me, Johnny. You tell me where the money is, and I'll get us out of here. We'll go away together. You won't regret it. That's a promise."

She shrugged out of the blouse and the vest. Bare to the waist, the dim light throwing soft shadows across her skin, she slid her open-fingered hands up across her breasts so that they swelled and bunched in her palms, then slipped down to bounce heavily when she let go.

She was watching him, not smiling, something on her face that he thought was defiance till he realized it was pride: pride in her body and how it could make her feel—how, using it, she could make a man feel. Her nipples were coming erect; he felt his mouth go dry, his throat tightening, felt himself begin to rise and thicken in response.

He swallowed to clear his throat. "A funny offer to make to me. I've seen what hanging around you has done to Red."

"You ain't like Red. You're strong. That's what I always liked about you. You can match me. We'd make a perfect team. You tell me where that ransom is, you wouldn't never have to worry about money again. I could set us up in a place—San Francisco, maybe, some big town where the business is good. I'm good at business. I could get enough girls working for us, it'd make that first forty thousand look like pin money."

"Dory, you're wasting your breath. I don't want nothing to do with you."

"You said that in Bowie. This is what told me you were lying then, too." And she reached down to cup the bulge at his crotch.

He tried to jerk away, but the ropes around his ankles held him tight, and her hand stayed with him, warm and firm, so that his movement only created friction, only aided her grasp, only made things worse.

"You may think I'm just trying to work on you," she said. "Trying to get that money. Well, I am. We both know that. But I mean everything else I'm saying, too. I always liked you better than any man I ever met. I always wished it was you that stuck with me instead of Red. We always made sparks together I never had with anybody else." Now she flipped the skirt up and swung a leg over to sit astraddle of him, her crotch pressed hot to his, her back arched, hands cupping her breasts. "Tell me where it is, Johnny. Let me get us out of here before it's too late."

"Dory, goddamn—don't . . ."

He writhed up against the ropes, trying to throw her off, but she clung to him with her thighs, riding him till he fell back onto the bed. She watched him with heavy-lidded eyes, her hips moving ever so slightly back and forth against him. Her face was flushed, her mouth open and slack; through the hot blood flooding his brain, he realized that she did mean everything she said, that making his blood hot made her own blood hot as well, and that she was perfectly capable and willing to set him up as some kind of fancy man, while she worked the girls and ran the business and brought the money in.

Now she started undoing the buttons up the side of her skirt, baring one shapely leg an inch at a time. "With that forty thousand, Johnny, we could start us a good house. Fancy. With velvet drapes and chandeliers and the best-looking girls in town. You wouldn't have to do anything. Just hang around and keep an eye on things. You could even take any of the girls upstairs, anytime you wanted. I wouldn't mind. We could even do it together. You and me and any girl we fancied. I'd like that. You've never lived in that kind of luxury, have you, Johnny? I have. The best clothes. The best food. The best liquor. A fancy carriage to ride around in, two or three girls on your arm. Let's do it, Johnny. Let's take that money for ourselves and go to San Francisco."

With what little thought he was still capable of he formed an image of himself after a few years of that kind of life: spineless, and weak, and drinking himself to death. Worse than Red. But he couldn't find his voice to reply.

Just then there was a rap on the back door. The guard—he didn't recognize the voice—said, "Dory? Dory, can you hear me?"

She had just undone the last button of the skirt; she halted in mid-movement, an edge of the waistband in either hand, the waistband itself parted to reveal one complete stripe of blond body laid bare: leg and thigh and naked flank, hip curving up into the swoop of her waist, slightly twisted now, breasts swaying sideways, as she turned toward the door.

"Sandy?"

"Dory? Ashe is coming. You better come out of there."

So it was Sandy Quinn, her lover. And likely Quinn even knew what she was doing in here. Dory was the kind of woman who could get a man to agree to that. She'd already proved with Red what she could get a man to put up with.

She turned to look down at him, sober-eyed. He felt her weight settle, saw the rise and fall of those big bare breasts as her breathing slowed, her nipples slowly shrinking. For one long moment she studied his face, anger coming into the set of her mouth. "I always liked you, Johnny. And I meant what I said. But you had your chance. I don't like getting told no a second time."

She swung off the bed; he saw an expanse of naked haunch as she pulled the waistband closed. She avoided his eyes as she slipped into the blouse and started buttoning it up, the look on her face that of an angry child.

When she was completely dressed again, the skirt buttoned up and the vest laced across her breasts, she flashed him one last angry look. "You won't hold out against Ashe. You'll talk. And you'll wish you'd talked to me when you could've." Then she crossed to the door and went out.

He sagged back on the mattress, feeling the blood beating at the back of his neck, feeling his breathing slowly subside. His arms hurt where her weight had forced them together behind his back, and his stomach was still fluttering from the memory of her warm soft body on his. She wasn't a girl anymore. He could attest to that, though he'd sensed in her at fifteen everything in the woman she had become, and he had shied away from it even then. She had only developed it more, learned that she could use it to get what she wanted. He had an inkling of what kept Red tagging at her heels, but a man would have to have a peculiar kind of kink not to see beneath the velvet glove to the iron hand within.

Ashe Greene wouldn't wear a velvet glove. And the question now was whether he could hold out against Greene and his bullyboys—whether he would have to fork over that ransom or could maybe find a way to trick them out of it. If what he suspected was true, likely they would kill him as soon as they had the money. So maybe the question was just whether he could hold out at all. He wasn't going to have to wait long to find out: He could already hear the sound of men coming up the path behind the cabins, the murmur of talk, the scuff of boots mounting the porch.

Then the latch rattled, and the door swung open.

12

Dooley and Fox stood in the doorway. He could see more men crowded up on the little porch behind them. Fox was carrying a shotgun; Dooley was empty-handed, but Slocum could see the gun belt under the Mexican poncho the man wore. Dooley crossed to the bunk and began untying the rope around Slocum's ankles.

"Ashe wants a little talk with you," he said. "You ain't going to like it, but that's what you get for being stubborn."

When his ankles were loose, Slocum sat up on the side of the bunk, flexing his legs to work the soreness out of them. His wrists were still bound behind his back, but at least his weight was off his arms and he could stretch some of the ache out of them, too. He saw the other man watching him from the porch. It was a little harder than he liked to admit to get himself to stand up and face them.

Dooley prodded him in the back, shoving him toward the door. "Outside. This is going to take some room."

The men at the door crowded back on the porch to let him through. Runnion was the only other man he recognized. He figured the tall one—blondish, with a young, almost too pretty face—was Sandy Quinn, but there were others he hadn't seen before, seven or eight of them altogether. Dooley prodded him down the steps and out onto the hard bare ground behind the cabin.

The sun had already set behind the high cliff on the west; the canyon was quiet and still in the early evening light. He saw no guard up on the slope below the mine shaft, but likely Ramona Warren was still in there.

There was no need for a guard with all these men down here in sight of the mine. They had followed him down off the porch, circling him now, watching him. He figured it was Ashe Greene they were waiting for and that it was Ashe Greene he saw down behind the second cabin, talking to Red and Dory. Warily, bracing himself, feeling awkward with his wrists bound behind him, he watched the three of them turn and start up the path along the back of the cabins.

Greene was tall and lean and black-haired, dressed in dingy jeans and scuffed boots worn down at the heels, a Colt slung low on one hip. Dory marched along at his side, head up, face flushed, looking angry and eager. Red tagged along behind them, watching the ground as though unwilling to meet Slocum's eyes.

The circle parted to let Greene through. Up close, Slocum saw he had a week's growth of beard. The man propped his hands on his hips, his slow grin revealing tobacco-stained teeth.

"So this is Boldt's messenger boy, is it?" He raked Slocum with a glance, as if to determine how strong he was, how much it might take to get him to talk. "Dory here tells me Boldt sent the ransom money out with you, but you somehow forgot where you put it. Is that right?"

"Dory said it," Slocum said. "Ask her."

Greene showed those tobacco-stained teeth again. "Now, is that a friendly answer? Red says you're a friend of his, says he wouldn't like to see you hurt. You ain't going to make that necessary, are you?"

Slocum looked at the men surrounding him. "Fuck you, Greene."

He saw Greene nod to somebody behind him, and before he could react, something slammed across the back of his knees. His legs went out from under him; he landed hard on his back, painfully wrenching his arms, legs instinctively drawing up to avoid another blow. For a moment he was too dazed to see; then he became aware of Fox standing over him, still gripping by the barrels the shotgun he had hit him with.

"That's just a taste," Greene said, and nodded to Fox again.

Slocum felt Fox seize him by the collar and drag him up to his knees. Rage blossomed somewhere down in his belly, and he staggered to his feet, head lowered, glaring at Greene, close to surprise at the heat he felt coming from his own eyes.

"You're going to talk," Greene said. "Better make it easy on yourself."

"Fuck you."

This time it was Dooley who hit him, wheeling from the side to sink a fist into his belly. Slocum had been expecting it, but even so it doubled him over, driving the wind out of him. For an instant he thought he was going to be sick; still bent at the waist he swayed on widespread feet, the ground spinning dizzily before his eyes, the hot taste of bile rising up into his throat.

"Please, Cap'n," Red said. "Don't let 'em do this to you."

That brought his head up. He didn't need any begging for mercy. Even by somebody else. He found Red's face in the circle, but Red looked away, something like shame in his eyes. Dory was watching him, though; her face had gone pale, but there was still anger there, still a hint of pleasure at watching this done to him.

Slocum spat bile onto the ground, feeling the heat returning to his eyes. "You'll be rotten meat before I'll talk, Greene. You're maybe used to yellowbellies like this bunch, but you'll never break me."

He didn't see who hit him this time. It came from the side again, a blow to the temple that stunned him; he felt himself reel back against another man, felt that man give him a kick to the kidney that drove him out into the center of the circle, where he lurched to gain his footing and wheeled, still dizzy but looking for where

the next blow would come from. Surprisingly, none
came. He planted himself solid, breathing hard, swinging his head from side to side, still expecting another
rush. Slowly, his vision cleared, and he saw Greene
grinning at him.

"It's only going to get worse," Greene said. "You'll
break. Better talk now and save us all a lot of trouble."

Seeing that grin brought rage rising up within him
again; he braced himself and spat at Greene this time.
"Fuck you."

Greene stepped in now, bringing a knee up toward
Slocum's groin. Slocum had been expecting it, hoping
for it; he twisted sideways, took the knee on his hip,
and drove a boot into Greene's other ankle, kicking him
to the ground. He wheeled in time to meet a rush from
Dooley, brought his own knee up into Dooley's crotch,
bounced off him to catch a blow beside his eye from
Quinn. Rage rushed up in him. He butted Quinn in the
belly, felt hands grab at his bound arms, pulling him
around, felt a boot take him in the knee, and then he
went down.

There was no defending himself anymore; he felt
blows beating him down—a boot to the head, another to
the side, another grazing off his elbows—and all he felt
was rage, rage and defiance. He was dimly aware of
Greene chanting "Talk . . . talk . . . talk" almost in
rhythm with the kicks, and dimly aware of a voice
saying "Fuck you" over and over, even more dimly
surprised to realize the voice was his own; and he knew
now that they would kill him before he talked, because
there was a point beyond which every blow only added
to his rage, where defiance became the only emotion he
was capable of, a point where the rage froze his brain
and wouldn't let him break even when he felt uncon-
sciousness coming.

He must have been out for a moment. When he came
to, the blows had stopped and he felt somebody ripping
the shirt from his back. He was lying on his face, still

barely conscious; he felt the shirt rip away, even the sleeves shredding down off his arms, and then he was bare to the waist, his head ringing, the taste of blood at the back of his mouth.

He heard Greene say, "Bring the latigo off that old saddle on the corral. We'll string him up to that porch roof and see how he likes a taste of leather."

Rage blossomed in him again. He rolled onto his side, struggled up to his knees, and swayed there, barely able to see, looking for Greene. He felt an almost animal hatred twisting his face—he wanted Greene; he still had strength enough to launch himself at Greene one more time.

"It won't work," Dory said. "I know Slocum. You've got his pride up. He'll die before he talks now. Bring her down here. Use the latigo on her. That'll make him talk."

He couldn't see her. All he saw was a blur, dizzy shapes. His head was thrumming like a steam engine.

"By God, I think you're right," Greene said. "Quinn, go bring that woman down here."

Slocum swayed on his knees, feeling consciousness come and go in waves; then somebody planted a boot in his back and shoved, and he sprawled down on his face again and let the dizziness overtake him, almost welcoming it, watching a thought take shape in the billowing blackness of his mind, like something separate from him, something he watched spelled out in faint letters in the dark, curiously bemused at what it eventually said: He would have died just now. Wherever that rage came from, it would have kept him defiant until he died. And in his almost pleasant floating state, drifting as he was from one edge of consciousness to the other, he couldn't decide whether that was a good thing or something bad, something that could almost explain why he'd spent his life the way he had, roaming from the Mississippi to the Rockies and beyond, always ready to take on a fight, whether it was somebody else's or his own.

"Get him up," Greene said. "Get him up where he can see."

He felt hands grab his arms, pull him back up on his knees. He crouched there, waves of dizziness still sweeping through him. His eyes were starting to focus; the ring of men had parted, and now he saw Sandy Quinn leading Ramona Warren down the slope from the mine.

She was barefoot, the hem of her dress brushing along the ground. They had taken the shackle off her leg, and Quinn was leading her at the end of a rope tied around her wrists. Tall, slim, long-legged, she walked with her head up, trying to look proud; but even through his dizziness Slocum could see how pale her face was against that wild sweep of red hair. Fear flickered in her eyes when she recognized him, bruised and bloody on the ground; then Quinn tossed the end of the rope up over a two-by-four connecting the studs just under the porch roof and mounted the steps to pull it tight.

Her eyes were on Slocum; the tug of the rope caught her off guard, yanked her off her feet and dragged her up against the edge of the porch. By the time she recovered her balance, Quinn had her strung up by her wrists, teetering on precarious tiptoe, breasts straining against the bodice of the dress.

Dory stepped up behind her, seized the collar of the dress with both hands, and ripped it all the way down to the waist, leaving only a thin cotton chemise beneath which those big breasts swelled round and taut, the nipples clearly visible.

"Ah, now, Dory, don't," Red said.

Dory turned, her face flushed again, eyes flashing. "If you're going to do this, do it right." And she reached up to rip the chemise down, stripping Ramona Warren naked to the waist.

Even as he fought to get his mind clear, Slocum sensed the hush that fell all around him, men made breathless but half ashamed by what they'd done. He saw Ramona Warren's frightened eyes flick toward him across one upward-straining arm, saw those huge breasts quivering and jiggling as Dory worked the dress down till it cascaded to the woman's ankles. She teetered there, on tiptoe, every muscle stretched taut, naked except for white satin pantalettes that came halfway down her thighs. Dory was just reaching for the pantalettes when Ashe Greene pulled her away.

"That's enough," Greene said, and stepped over to take her place, the latigo, a leather strap about two inches wide, dangling from his hand.

Slocum struggled to his feet, ribs aching, eyes still a little blurred. "All right," he said. "All right, I'll talk."

Dooley shoved him toward Greene. "You better make it quick."

"I stashed the ransom," Slocum said. "On the way out. It's in a canvas bag. Under that bridge about halfway to town."

Greene drew his Colt and brought the muzzle of it up within an inch of Slocum's eyes, anger showing on his face for the first time. "You better be telling the truth. Because you're going to wait here till we get back. And if we ain't found that money, you're going to wish we'd killed you just now." And with one fast move, he whipped the Colt up and brought the barrel of it down on Slocum's head.

13

He had no idea how long he was out. He came to with a start, thrashing up out of blackness; then he realized he was back on the bunk, in the cabin, his wrists still bound behind him. And not alone.

The cabin was dark. Not yet fully conscious, he sensed soft skin against his chest, a cloud of hair on the mattress beside his head, a face an inch away. Ramona Warren. He tried to struggle up again.

"It's no use," she whispered. "We're tied together around the waist."

His eyes were adjusting to the dark. Moonlight seeped through the chinks in the log walls, and now he saw light coming from the cracks around the door—somebody had a lantern on the back porch. He arched backward at the waist, far enough to get a look at her, and even in that faint light he could see something close to a blush on her face.

They had tied her hands behind her back as well. And they had put her on the bunk just as she was. Except for those thin satin pantalettes, she was stark naked.

Her bound arms were forcing her back into an arch, thrusting her breasts out almost unnaturally large and round toward him. And now he became aware of the heat of her lower body, pressed tight against him by the rope around their waists. Their knees and ankles were bound together too.

"Dory's idea," she said. "Greene and Dooley tied us up, but she supervised."

He couldn't hold that backward arch long. He gave it up, the rope bringing him back against her. He felt her breasts soften and swell against his bare chest, heard her breathing close beside his ear, felt the smooth warm flesh of her belly against his own.

"It's all right," she said. "Not your fault. I don't know what happened, but you tried. You'll just have to put up with me this way till they get back."

And he felt her nipples hardening against his chest.

He reared back to look at her again. She wore a faint, almost apologetic smile. She glanced down at her breasts, where her twin nipples stood out hard and erect. "I'm sorry. I can't help it. You have to admit we're going to get to know each other very well in here like this. They won't be back till morning at least."

"We got to find some way out of here before they get back. Because I didn't hide that money where I told them."

The smile left her face then. "Oh."

The strain was too much; he released the arch and came back against her again. "I worked a nail out away from the bedstead when I was in here before," he said, his face up against hers. "It's behind me. You'll have to scoot this way. There's a chance I can work these ropes loose or shred them on that nail tip."

He could feel her breath against his face when she spoke: "You'll have to be careful. There's guards on both porches."

"How long was I out? Have they come in here since Greene and the rest rode out?"

"It's been more than an hour. I think there are only two left. And I heard Greene give them strict orders to stay outside. I think he was a little squeamish about this, but Dory persuaded him."

They were whispering, their mouths barely an inch apart. He could feel her hair against the side of his face.

In this sudden enforced intimacy she seemed suddenly someone he knew, someone he could trust, someone friendly. She was right: Bound together as they were, all pretense stripped away with most of their clothes, whispering together to find a way out of an unexpected common predicament, they were going to get to know each other very well very quickly. Oddly, the thought brought a slow stirring to his groin; he felt himself begin to harden and come erect.

She felt it too. He could tell by the way her pelvis pressed against his as if to confirm there what she'd sensed. Now her nipples grew hard against his chest again, and this time it was she who drew away to look at his face.

"I guess I'm not the only one," she said.

Her backward arch was pressing her groin even tighter against his, increasing the pressure there, her breasts swelling full and taut. Not smiling, she examined his face with sober eyes, as if to read his thoughts.

"Sorry," he said. "Natural response. Can't help it."

"I know. Neither can I. I feel a little strange. Promise me something, will you?"

"What's that?"

"If we get out of here, don't take me straight back to Sam. We'll know each other very well by then. I think we deserve some time together."

"I thought you were planning to become the man's wife."

She came down against him, her mouth seeking his, warm and wet, and he felt her tongue soft against his own. "I went with enough men to make him money," she whispered. "If I'm going to settle down, I want one last time with somebody I want, for pleasure. And he could have got me killed trying to hold off paying. It'll serve him right for caring more for his money than for me."

The offer inflamed him. Her breasts were softened

against his chest again, making his palms itch with the urge to stroke them. "I told him I'd bring you back within a week. If we get away from here, we should have plenty of time to spend together."

"Good. Now where's that nail?"

He reached back with his bound hands, seized the bunk frame, and levered himself toward it, pulling her with him. He found the nail sticking out of the wood and hooked it into the ropes at his wrists, trying to cut through a strand. The strain on his shoulders was tremendous; the weight of Ramona's body kept pulling him away from the nail, and he couldn't avoid awareness of her warm pelvis pressed tight to his own.

He felt one strand of the rope break, and then he relaxed, sagging back against her. "You'll have to roll this way," he whispered. "Roll over on top of me." Then he reached back for the nail again.

This time she rolled all the way over, so that he was almost on his back on the edge of the bunk. The rope around their waists held her half on her side, anchoring him; he could feel one big breast pillowed against his chest, the soft flesh between her thighs yielding as he arched to work at the nail again.

It seemed to take forever. He could hold that arch for only a few minutes at a time, groping for the nail, hooking the tip of it into the ropes, straining to cut through another strand. Then he would relax, sag back against her, trying to keep his breathing quiet, listening for suspicious sounds from the guards on the porches. Each time he relaxed, he would find her eyes on him in the dim light, sober and reflective, as if seeking in his face a reaffirmation of that friendly mood they had established earlier, as if she needed that to dispel any embarrassment she might feel. And each time he would feel her nipples begin to come erect again, would feel himself begin to harden against the yielding flesh between her thighs, would hear her breathing quicken, her eyes steadily on his for reassurance. It was like a form of torture; every time he reared back, he would feel his hardness probing into her, and only the strain on his shoulders would eventually dissipate it, let him concentrate enough to work on the nail. And then he would relax back against her and it would start all over again.

It was more than an hour before he began to feel the knot loosen. He hadn't cut it. He had picked at it for the better part of the hour, digging the point of the nail in and catching it, jerking at it, trying either to break through a strand or pull an end of the rope free. It seemed a very long time before he felt it even move, and longer still before he knew the knot was going to come loose. He got the nail in between the loops of the rope, pulled one free, probed till he worked another out, and then another. Then the rope fell from his wrists, and he swung his arms around, his shoulders aching from the strain, and let himself relax against her again.

"You did it," she whispered.

He felt the smooth skin of her waist under his hand. He traced the rope around their waist till he found the knot, at the small of her back, and fumbled it loose. And then the ropes binding her wrists together.

When they were both free, only their legs still bound, she brought her hands up to rub his upper arms, stroking the ache away. She was still breathing hard from the strain; he felt her breasts swell and subside against his chest, felt the satiny skin of her back smooth under his hands, and now that slow heat returned to his groin, hardening him again, digging him into the soft flesh between her thighs. She ran her hands up the back of his neck, bringing his mouth to hers, and again he felt the soft wet touch of her tongue. She moved against him, pushing her hips into his.

"You deserve a kiss," she murmured.

"Later. Now we got to find a way out of this cabin."

Quickly, he untied the ropes around their legs and shifted to the edge of the bunk. Light still came through the cracks at the front door, but the back was dark. Maybe that guard back there had got bored; maybe he had carried his lantern around to sit and palaver with the man in front. He got to his feet and crept carefully to the back door.

For a long moment he heard nothing. Then he heard a faint sound, a man shifting his position on the porch. The guard had maybe doused his lantern, but he was still there. Slocum turned and crept back to the bunk.

Ramona had risen to sit on the edge of it, hands up in a vain attempt to cover those big breasts. Even in these circumstances he had to restrain an urge to sink back on the mattress with her, to satisfy the itch that had been tormenting him for over an hour.

"We'll have to go up the chimney," he whispered. "I think it's big enough inside. You think you can make it?"

"I think so."

He crept across to the rock fireplace and crouched down to stick his head inside. He could see a square of pale light at the top of the chimney: the moonlit sky. The chimney was crudely built out of rocks of different shapes and sizes; there should be plenty of handholds on the way up.

He felt a hand on his back and turned to see her crouching beside him. "I'll go up first," he said. "Wait till you see me clear the top, then start up after me. And try not to make any noise."

Then he stood upright in the chimney, felt with his boot for a foothold, reached to seize an outcropping of rock overhead, and hauled himself upward.

It was slow going. He had to test each foothold, unable to tell through the leather of the boot just how much of a grip it would provide. Years of accumulated

ash made the handholds slippery; thick clouds of soot
rained down on his face, stinging his eyes and choking
his mouth. He had to halt every foot or so to wipe it
away. Once he slipped, his foot going out from under
him; he caught himself quickly, but his scrabble for
purchase had sounded very loud, and he crouched there,
each boot braced against a wall of the chimney, listening. When he was sure the sound hadn't carried, he
blew the soot away from his mouth and continued on.

It seemed forever before his hands encountered the
top of the chimney and he hoisted himself up and out,
into the warm night. He lowered himself gently onto the
slanting roof and knelt there, grateful for the fresh air.

The lantern was casting a dim glow across the ground
in front of the cabin. The back was still dark. Lamplight
came from the windows of the first cabin, at the other
end of the row. He figured that would be the Mex
woman. In the moonlight he could see two horses in the
corral. One of those was the gray. Too risky trying to
get in there, but there was a saddled horse tethered to
the rail just outside the corral gate. Two horses that he
could see, other than the gray; that likely meant only
two men still here. Likely everybody else had headed
for the bridge; nobody wanted to be missing when the
money was counted. He rose to look back down the
chimney.

Ramona was almost to the top; he saw the white of
her face as she looked up, searching for another hand-
hold. In another moment her hands came out, then her
head, and she hauled herself halfway out and paused to
rest, elbows braced on the edges of the chimney mouth.
He seized her by the waist and lifted her out onto the
roof.

She leaned against him, breathing hard, big bare
breasts pillowed against his chest. "What now?"

"Stay here. I want to check those guards."

Testing each foothold to make sure no shingle

squeaked, one slow and quiet step at a time, he crept along the slant of the roof toward the back porch. He wanted to see where that guard was. If he could catch the man unawares, he might be able to drop on him, knock him out, and get his gun. The guard in the front would hear it, but it would be one-on-one then—it was worth the risk. When he neared the edge of the roof, he lowered himself carefully to his hands and looked down over the eave.

The guard was back up under the porch, not even in sight. For a moment, he considered trying it anyway—he would have surprise; he could maybe drop and tackle the man before he got a gun unlimbered. Then, looking off down the row, he spotted another horse tethered behind the first cabin. Three men, then; one to spell these two on guard shifts. Not very good odds. And with that lantern throwing light up toward the opposite cabin, where he'd hidden that canvas sack, it was for sure he couldn't get to that money now. Best try to sneak out of here, and then wait till morning. When the rest got back and found him and Ramona gone, thinking they had the money, likely the whole crew would ride out of this canyon to try and run them down. He could slip back in then, get that money sack with no trouble at all. He rose and worked his way quietly back along the roof.

Ramona was crouched down beside the chimney, hands pressed to her breasts. Her skin was nearly as white as the pantalettes she wore; she looked totally naked in the moonlight. He knelt down beside her, scooped some soot out of the chimney, and began smearing it across his chest.

"Still a guard on each end," he whispered. "We'll have to try dropping off the side. There's grass there. We should be able to do it."

She was watching him smear the soot along his arms. "What's that for?"

"I want to get to that horse by the corral. We'll be crossing fifty yards of open ground, in the moonlight. The darker we are, the better. You look white as ivory."

She looked down at her breasts spilling out around her hands. Then back at him. Again he sensed that need for reassurance. Whatever she saw in his face made it all right—she reached into the chimney, breasts suddenly swinging free, brought out a double handful of soot, and began spreading it across her stomach.

He was blackening his face when she started on her breasts. Watching, he felt dryness tighten his throat. She was so slender, so long-legged, so beautiful with that flare of red hair framing her face. And so naked. Her breasts bobbled and lurched through her palms as she smeared the soot across them. Her nipples were erect; he couldn't tell if it was from the night air. He wasn't aware that his own hands had stopped till he saw that she was studying his face.

She leaned up to kiss him. "If you don't stop looking at me like that we won't get off this roof."

"I think you're right," he said, and reached for another handful of soot.

When she had finished blackening her legs and arms and had rubbed the pantalettes as dark as she could get them, he turned so that she could do his back. Then he blackened hers, his palms brought alive by her sleek smooth skin, the curves of her shoulder blades, the swoop of her waist. He spread the soot up the back of her neck while she did her face; when he was through, she turned, black as any slave out of the Old South, and cuddled up in his arms.

He whispered in her ear, "Who was it said something about getting off this roof?"

"Just comfort me a minute. I feel funny. Scared and excited at the same time. I need to be held."

He held her up against him, feeling those big breasts squashing against his chest. He could feel the heat of her through his jeans, and the answering stir from himself. He figured Boldt was a lucky man—and a smart one: Dory for Ramona was a good trade.

After a moment, she touched his face and moved away. "I'm ready."

Together, they crept quietly down the roof. The corral was fifty yards straight north of the cabin. Slocum got down on his belly and peered over the edge. It was a good ten-foot drop, but the ground looked soft there, where the rain runoff had built up a thick stand of grass. He figured they could make it. Carefully, he eased around till he could lower himself down off the eave. When he was hanging by his hands, he let himself go and dropped.

He landed in the soft grass under the eaves, just catching himself against the side of the cabin. He crouched there for a moment, listening, wishing he had a gun. No sound came from either end of the cabin. He rose to his feet and looked up.

Black as she was, Ramona was barely visible, lying flat at the edge of the roof. He signaled that it was safe, and she began edging around, her legs coming down off the roof one by one; he could see her arms shaking from the strain as she lowered one hand to grip the eave, then the other. Then she released her hold, and he caught her around the waist as she fell.

She slid down against him, trembling. He held her close, ears straining for noise from the ends of the cabin. Nothing.

"Now's the hard part," he whispered. "Keep low and quiet. Don't run. We'll circle around the corral and come up on the horse from behind. We don't want to spook it."

He took her hand, and they began to creep through the grass to the north of the cabin.

After twenty yards, he crouched down in the grass and looked back. The guard on the front porch was silhouetted against the glow of the lantern. The man in back was just a vague form in the moonlight. If either of them looked this way, they might see movement, but he and Ramona were dark as the night. As long as they made no noise, they should be all right. He rose from his crouch, and they started on.

It took ten minutes till he figured they were far enough into the dark not to be seen. They had passed by the corral; now he left Ramona huddled in the grass and started back toward it, coming up along the near side, where the saddled horse was tethered, working his way along the rail one foot at a time. This side of the corral was directly in line with the front porch; he could be seen from here. He slipped in between the rail and the horse, stroking the horse's neck to keep it quiet, and edged up to untie the reins. The guard was hunkered down against the door; pray to God he had his eyes closed. The back corner of the cabin put the other man out of sight. Slocum eased the horse around and led it slowly back into the dark.

When he got back to where Ramona was, he untied the bedroll behind the saddle, laid it out on the ground, and started searching around the bottom of it. Ramona crept over to him, hugging herself, breasts cradled in the embrace of her arms.

"What are you doing?" she whispered.

"Whoever this horse belongs to travels light. Most men like that carry an extra handgun in their bedroll. That, and whatever else they'll need on the trail."

His hands encountered a set of spurs, a small box, then another, then something soft that turned out to be the man's spare shirt. "Here," he said. "Put that on." Then he found what he was looking for—a Colt .45. One of the boxes contained ammunition. He loaded the Colt and shoved it down in his waistband. There was a Winchester in the saddle sheath, but a rifle was too unwieldy. There might be a man posted on the bluff at the north end of the canyon, and he was going to have his hands full guiding the horse up that rocky trail.

Ramona had the shirt on and buttoned up to her neck. Slocum slung the bedroll back on behind the saddle and lashed it down tight. Then he mounted up, reached down a hand to help her up behind him, and started up through the dark, keeping the horse at a walk to avoid making noise.

14

He had no trouble finding the break in the pines where the trail started up the cliff face. A rock slide had deposited a pile of loose shale there, brighter than the dark trees on either side of it. He spurred up through the shale, found the beginning of the ledge that led upward, and kneed the reluctant horse out onto it. The ledge was a good ten feet wide here—plenty of room. But there were those breaks he remembered farther up, at least one place where a rock slide had taken a good chunk of the trail down with it. That was where it would get tricky.

Ramona clung to his waist; he felt her hands clasped across his belly above his belt buckle, her breasts soft against his back. He could tell by the tightness of her grip that she was scared, but she didn't say anything.

The ledge climbed at a steep angle, narrowing gradually. Likely it was an Indian trail; from the signs, it hadn't been used in a long time. The moon brightened the cliff face, solid rock all the way up, with none of the tree growth there had been near the top of the south face coming in. He tried to avoid looking down.

He figured they were about halfway up the bluff when he saw the first rock slide ahead. Most of the ledge had broken away, leaving a cracked and jagged shelf barely a yard wide. They would have to cross it on foot, and the horse would have a hard time of it even without anybody on its back—if what was left of the ledge would hold at all.

"We'll have to dismount. You hold the horse still. I'll go see if it's safe."

He left her holding the reins and eased his way out onto the ledge, putting one careful foot in front of the other, hugging the cliff on his right. He reached the far end with no sign of trouble. Secure enough to hold a man, anyway. A horse might be a different matter. He turned and worked his way back.

"You first," he said. "I'll follow. If it can't hold the horse, at least you'll be across."

She touched a hand to his waist, her eyes on his. "Be careful."

"It's not too wide. If it goes, likely I can jump."

She faded off into the dark, barely visible with the dark soot covering her skin. When he was sure she was across, he clucked the horse and started after her.

The horse balked, head rearing up against the pull of the reins. He led it out a step at a time, one hand pulling on the reins, the other braced against the cliff. He saw the white of its eyes in the moonlight, saw it test the ground in front with each delicate hoof, trembling, blowing, nostrils flaring. He kept his back to the cliff, one eye on the horse, the other on Ramona crouched just beyond the end of the break. The ledge was just wide enough, the saddle scraping against the rock face. Small chunks of rock jarred loose along the edge and skittered away down into the darkness. The drop was close to perpendicular here; a fall would take him all the way to the bottom.

He was almost to the end of the break when he heard the ledge begin to crack and crumble behind him.

The horse squealed, eyes wild. Slocum dived for solid ground, yanking on the reins, hearing the desperate scramble of hooves as the ledge began to break away under the horse's hindquarters. He knew he should let it go, but he braced himself and heaved. The ledge crumbled and fell away. The horse arched and lunged; its rear hooves caught the edge of the break, and it scrambled up, lurched out onto secure footing, and stood there, trembling violently.

Slocum's heart was beating like a war drum; he stroked the horse's neck, waiting for his own nerves to settle down. "Close," he said. "We'll go on afoot from here. I think there's another rock slide farther up. I'll lead. I doubt if they expect anybody to use this trail, but we can't chance finding a guard at the top."

The next rock slide was easier. The trail narrowed to no more than a yard again, and he had to coax the spooked horse across, but even the broken part of the ledge held. He drew his Colt when they neared the top, but his hunch was correct—there was no guard. He led the horse up over the edge of the cliff, out onto a flat bluff covered with scrub grass and stunted pines.

"Where to now?" Ramona said.

"You said Greene told those guards to stay out of the cabin till he got back. That'll be dawn at the earliest. When they find us gone, likely the whole bunch will ride out looking for us. They'll think we've got the ransom, only I hid it under one of those cabins. I figure we should bed down tonight and slip back in to get it tomorrow, when they've left the canyon empty. That all right with you?"

"Anything you say." She was standing close, smiling at him, her face a dull black under the soot. "We did promise ourselves some time together."

"We did, didn't we." He heard his voice go husky at the thought of it. "Let's go, then."

In the saddle again, Ramona up behind him, he headed northwest at a walk. Greene's bunch would figure they had set out for Bowie, and this route took them away from town; they shouldn't have to go far to put a safe distance behind them.

The country on this side of the canyons was more wooded, sloping gradually to the north; in an hour they were in a stand of tall pines, and half an hour after that they came out of the tree line onto a level stretch of ground, a grassy glade running along a little river. It looked as good a place as any; at least there was water to wash that soot off.

He reined in under the branches of a tree about twenty yards from the river's edge, dismounted, and helped Ramona down. Then he untied the bedroll from behind the saddle and threw it down at the base of the tree.

"Look through that. Generally, a man carries a bar of lye soap around with him. We can get this soot off before bed."

While she unrolled the bedroll on the grass and started searching through it, he removed the horse's bridle and hung it on a limb. He didn't take the saddle off, just loosened the cinch. If Greene somehow found them, they might have to leave here in a hurry, and he didn't want to lose the time it would take to saddle up again.

Ramona was removing things from the bottom of the bedroll: the spare spurs, an extra set of reins, the boxes of .45 ammunition. He crouched down beside her just as she came up with a bar of soap.

"Put all that other stuff to the side," he said. "We can repack it in the morning. You go clean up. I want to take care of this horse."

She was kneeling on the grass, legs gleaming a dull black in the moonlight, her eyes very white in the dark of her face. She leaned across to kiss him, her breasts shifting heavily under the thin shirt. "Will you come soap me down?" she said.

He felt his breath catch in his throat. "We start that, it'll take a long time getting that soot off."

"I'd like that. Remember, this is my last time before I get married."

"We got hours. And there's nothing I'd like better. You go on. I'll be with you in a minute."

He watched her cross the stretch of moonlight toward the little river and put the soap down on the grassy bank. She stripped off the shirt and dropped it beside the soap, then bent to step out of the soot-smeared pantalettes. He caught a flash of white thighs, white buttocks, then she picked up the soap and stepped naked down off the bank. He made himself look away.

He still ached in a dozen places from the beating he'd taken, but he hardly felt it through that hungry surge rising up within him. After Dory's performance that afternoon, after going through what he had with Ramona, both of them half naked as they were, it would take more than a beating to kill that hunger. He forced himself to concentrate, fashioning a pair of hobbles out of the extra set of reins, then leading the hobbled horse off along the tree line to get it away from the campsite. When he was certain the hobbles were secure, he left the horse grazing at the edge of the trees and crossed the glade to where she had dropped the shirt.

The river widened into a little pool here, shallow at the edges. She stood about five yards out from the bank, in water halfway up to her thighs, her back to him. She had almost finished soaping her body, but she was still dark with soot—wet now, and gleaming in the moonlight. He was struck by how tall she was, her long shapely legs rising up to high firm buttocks, white against the rest of her. Her slim waist cut sharply in above her hips, and her breasts were so large he could see each of them bulging out on either side, bobbling and quivering as she soaped one outstretched arm.

He couldn't watch any longer. He shucked his clothes and stepped off the bank, ducked underwater and came up streaming. He could tell she'd heard the splash, but she didn't turn around. He waded up behind her, already erect, already feeling the heaviness of it swinging at his groin. He slipped his hands around her soapy waist, her sleek wet back cradled against him.

"Thought you were going to wait for me to soap you down."

She ducked her head half around, a pleased smile just visible in the dark. "I wanted to be all slippery when you got here."

She turned, sliding that slippery body around in his arms, her breasts pillowing up against his chest. She was soapy all down the front as well; she propped her hands on his shoulders, still clutching the soap, and leaned back at the waist, watching his eyes as her groin came up warm and insistent against his. She spread her legs and arched her hips up, and he felt the hard erect length of him pressed into the folds of soft flesh between her thighs, slipping through the soapy curls there. She was so tall he had only to move his own hips once and he slid right up into her, into that hot moist tunnel he'd been so hungering to feel close around him. A little sound came from her throat, a little breathy gasp, and she rocked her head forward till all he could see was red hair and the nape of her neck, looking down to where he was sunk up in her. He gripped her waist and started to move, and now he felt her shift her weight on the river bottom, her feet inching outward for a better grip. He reared slowly back, till only the tip of him was in her, then sank back in again, slow and deep, and held there, feeling her quivering up against him. Her head came up till her eyes met his; for a long moment she gazed at him as they rocked back and forth; a little way out, a little way in; longer out, deeper in; and then her hands slid down to grip his waist and she leaned slowly back till her face was turned to the sky, exposing the long delicate line of her throat, her huge breasts arching upward, erect nipples pointing right at him, her haunches beginning to pump in rhythm with his own, those little sounds coming from her throat now with every move she made.

He couldn't bear this much longer; he seized her around the waist, lifted her off her feet; for a moment she arched backward in his arms, impaled on him, then her hands grabbed the nape of his neck and her legs came up to lock around his back, and he turned to wade toward the bank. She didn't cease to writhe in his arms. Eyes fiercely closed, lower lip clutched between her teeth, she rocked and rocked against him, haunches pumping up and down, huge breasts jiggling heavily against his chest, those frantic little cries escaping from her throat. He barely made it to the bank before his legs gave way and he sank to his knees on the grass at the river's edge, his feet still in the water, still gripping her around the waist as she plunged up and down and up and down. He felt himself almost involuntarily lunging up to meet her, surging upward, unable to restrain it, feeling her thighs writhing around him, the planes of muscle at the small of her back flexing under his hands; he sensed his own rhythm driving her on, on and up, till with one wild writhing lurching lunge he felt her soar over that barrier she'd been trying to clear, bringing him after, and they collapsed on the grass, him rolling onto his side, her hands still gripping the base of his neck, her legs still locked around his back, both of them still quivering and jerking, subsiding into quiet only to twitch involuntarily up again, trembling in the long lingering aftermath of what had just passed.

After a long while she snaked her arms up around his neck and put her hot wet mouth on his. When she drew away, he saw she was smiling. "That was worth everything we went through. Everything I went through, anyway."

"I'd go through a lot for that, myself."

She ran a hand down his ribs, slippery from the soap that had rubbed off her. "I guess I couldn't ask for a better time before I stand up in front of that preacher." She rolled away to lie on her back, stretching her arms up above her head, big breasts coming up taut, her feet dangling off the bank. She was still smeared with soap, streaks of pale skin showing through the soot. "Men always have that," she said. "A party before the wedding. Go out and get drunk and end up in a whorehouse. I've seen enough of them in my time. This was my party."

Watching her spread out naked like that he could feel

lingering hunger stirring within him. "What do you mean—was?"

She came up on one elbow to study his face, a small smile starting at the corners of her mouth. "You mean the party's not over?" She glanced down to where he was already beginning to thicken and swell again. "Oh, my, it's not over, is it?" And she reached down to take him in her hand, watching his face with that slowly spreading smile.

"I had you and Dory both stirring me up on that bunk today. And once is never enough. Besides, how many times do you have a party before getting married?" He grinned and gently removed her hand. "I want to get this soot off first."

She fell back on the grass, a little ripple of mirth running through her. "I lost the soap somewhere in the middle of all that. I don't know where."

He waded through the water till he found the soap, about ten feet out, and turned back toward the bank. Ramona had slid down into the water; she was propped against the bank, kneeling in the water, her elbows resting on the grass.

"I thought you were going to wash off," she said.

"Thought you might need some soap."

"Break me off a piece. But I want to watch." She cocked her head at him. "Can't I watch you? It's my party."

"Do what you want. I'm going to get clean."

He broke off half the soap and tossed it to her, then waded out into deeper water and went under, swimming out to the middle of the pool. The moon was almost directly overhead now; he could see a dense stand of pines on the opposite bank, a wooded ridge receding up into the dark. He turned, treading water, and swam back to where he could stand in the shallows; then started soaping himself down.

Ramona had already covered herself with soap. She knelt at the water's edge, running her hands slowly over her slippery body, watching him. He felt himself begin to harden and rise, heaviness dangling out from his groin. In the moonlight he could just make out the pleased smile on her face.

"You make a nice picture," she said.

"You make a pretty nice picture yourself."

She looked down at herself, slid her hands up to cup those huge breasts, creating a startling cleavage. Impulsively, he pitched the soap up onto the grass and went to kneel beside her, seizing her by the hair and pulling her head back and running a hand down into the soapy curls between her widespread thighs. The water came up just above her knees; she leaned back over the edge of the bank, eyes closed, her arms going up behind her head till she was arched backward like a bow, huge breasts thrusting up and quivering heavily each time her body twitched in response to his touch. He slid his hand farther down into the folds of that soft flesh, one finger slipping into her, and she tried to lurch away, held fast by his grip on her hair, by her own reluctance to lose contact with his fingers. She was clutching the grass with outflung hands, trembling, writhing, jerking upward with every stroke of his fingers. Those sounds were coming from her throat again, and now her thighs sagged even farther apart, her hips beginning to undulate—slowly, powerfully.

"Please," she gasped. "Please. Do it to me. Do it to me."

He swung in between her thighs, thrusting deep into her. Her legs came up to lock around the small of his back. He braced his hands on her outflung wrists, pinning her to the ground, plunging slowly into her and slowly out again, made something close to drunk by the sight of that voluptuous body squirming beneath him, her slim waist twisting as her haunches arched up to meet his thrusts, her huge heavy breasts bobbing and bouncing as her whole upper body squirmed on the grass. He sank down against her, feeling all those slippery curves and swells writhing against his skin, rolled onto his side, and brought his hands in to seize her by the waist, feeling her own arms sliding around his neck.

She lurched over against him, rolled him onto his back, and rose on hands and widespread knees, crouched above him, eyes closed, rocking steadily back and forth, breasts sliding heavily along his chest, stone-hard nipples raking his skin. He tightened his grip on her waist and drove up into her, meeting each lunge of her hips with a lunge of his own, and now her head came up, that wild red hair flaring around her face, exposing the long delicate line of her throat again, and she began to pump faster, faster, faster, husky sounds coming from deep within her. Suddenly she reared upright, face turned up to the sky, back arching upward, arms falling helplessly away till only his tight grip kept her from lunging right off him, and she seemed to lose all control, lurching and lunging up and down like a rider on a bucking horse, huge breasts tossing and heaving; she loosed one long deep guttural cry and collapsed down onto him, seizing his shoulders as her haunches pumped out that last wild frantic burst of pleasure.

It seemed a long time till all her quivering and twitching had stopped. She was sprawled on him, all restraint gone, long legs dangling down off the bank, her head laid against his. After a while she slid down onto her side, taking some of her weight off him, but he was still erect, still hard, still lodged deep inside her.

Feeling herself caught there, she placed a hand on his chest, her head sagging down into the hollow of his arm; there was something like wonder in her voice: "Does that mean what I think it means?"

He chuckled. "This is a special party, isn't it? Sooner or later, if we keep this up, we'll get all this soap and soot off."

It was another hour before they made it back to the bedroll. As he settled into it, feeling her long cool body pressed against his back, huge breasts pillowed up against him, one slim hand still stroking the flat of his belly in gratitude, he thought of Samuel Boldt and wondered how the man had survived to the age he had. If Dory Baker and Ramona Warren were any sign of his taste in women, Sam Boldt should have died of exhaustion long ago.

15

Sunlight on his face brought him awake. He stirred in the bedroll, sore and aching in a dozen places from the kicking he'd gotten the day before, and opened his eyes. He was unhappy to see the sun already high in the sky; he had planned to get up at dawn, but all that exertion had run his inner clock down, and from the look of the sun it was close to noon.

He heard soft footsteps behind him, and he became simultaneously aware that there was no body next to his. He turned in the bedroll and saw Ramona standing in the grass under a tree about ten yards away.

She was stark naked, in direct sunlight, stretching up on widespread tiptoe to feel at the damp shirt and pantalettes she had evidently washed out and draped over the tree limb to dry. She was half turned away from him, so that his eyes followed the shapely curves of her legs up to the firm round cheeks of her ass, then up the slender swoop of her waist to where those astonishingly big breasts swayed below her outstretched arms. The sight of her nearly took his breath away; he threw off the top cover and started to sit up.

She heard him and looked around. A sudden blush spread across her face and she dropped abruptly to her knees, crouching on the grass, one knee raised to conceal the curly triangle between her thighs, both arms cradled across her breasts in a vain attempt to cover all that soft round flesh spilling out around them.

He stifled a laugh. "You're embarrassed? After last night?"

Laughter bubbled up through her own confusion, but

the blush didn't go away. "I know it's silly, but this is different. It's broad daylight. I hardly know you."

"Hardly know me? I'd say you know me pretty well. And I can't be the only stranger that's seen you in the light."

Now she did laugh. "You're different. I don't feel like I did last night with a man who's paying. I don't let myself feel that way. Humor me."

"I don't know," he said. "I kind of like watching you like that."

She was laughing helplessly now, but still embarrassed, arms still trying to contain her breasts. "Please? Just look away for a minute? I'll come join you in that bedroll if you do."

He had just kicked the bedroll open, about to take her up on it, when he heard a distant shout, barely audible, far up beyond the wooded ridge they had descended the night before. He halted in mid-movement, braced on one hand, head cocked up the slope, listening hard. He heard only silence. That didn't mean anything; the top of that bluff was a good three miles away, but a freak breeze could sometimes carry a sound a long way down a mountainside.

Ramona was still crouching on the grass, but her face had gone pale. She had heard it too, and she knew as well as he did who it was.

He came up out of the bedroll and grabbed his boots and jeans. "That's got to be Greene's bunch. They must have tracked the horse away from the corral They can't have come up that trail, not with the ledge broken away, but I'll bet that was the lead man picking up our tracks at the top of it. I don't know if they can track us down through those pines, but we can't stay here."

Ramona had leaped to snatch her laundry off the tree limb. She had the pantalettes on and was just buttoning up the shirt when he finished dressing. He shoved the Colt into his waistband and grabbed the bridle off the limb he'd hung it on the night before.

"Stash those ammunition boxes in that bedroll and tie it up tight. We may need them, and we got nothing else to carry them in." And he set out at a run toward where the horse was grazing fifty yards down the river bank.

She had the bedroll rolled up and tied together when he led the horse back. He had already tightened up the saddle cinch; now he lashed the bedroll on behind, swung into the saddle, and reached down to help her up behind him.

"Where'll we go?" she said.

"Anywhere, so long as it's away from them. We got to lose them before we can do anything else."

He headed west along the river bank, the horse at a canter. If Greene lost the trail, he might figure they had cut back east, toward Bowie. In any case, they were already west of the point where that trail came out of the canyon; to turn east would only be losing ground.

The timber reached right down to the river's edge after about a hundred yards; he reined left up under the cool pines along the slope. He had to slow to a trot here, dodging around tree trunks, but at least the pine needles on the ground would muffle the sound of the horse. When they'd gone half a mile, he reined to a halt, listening back the way they'd come. He couldn't hear anything. But if Greene's bunch still had the trail, they would be descending through a bed of pine needles too. He kicked the horse on through the trees.

They stayed at a trot for close to two miles, sticking close to the river, reining up every half mile or so to listen. Ramona hadn't said a word since they'd left their campsite, just clung to his waist and dodged the tree limbs passing overhead. He didn't know what he would do if Greene's bunch caught up with them. There was that Winchester in the scabbard under the saddle cinch, but one rifle wouldn't do much good against a bunch that size.

The ground was sloping toward the west now. The

trees had begun to thin out. After another two hundred yards they gave out altogether, and he reined up at the edge of the tree line, looking off across a patch of greasewood toward a flat expanse of desert, barren as the country out from Bowie. No cover there, and anyway he wanted to get back into that canyon. He was about to rein around, thinking to climb the slope and skirt along the top of that bluff, when he heard the whinny of a horse somewhere behind him. Too close—and likely headed this way.

"Give me that Winchester," he said.

Ramona leaned down to slide the rifle out of its scabbard and passed it up to him.

"Now hang on," he said, and reined north down the slope, aiming for the river.

They hit it at a run, splashing out till the horse sank to its flanks and began to swim, struggling against a surprisingly swift current. Slocum had the reins in one hand, the rifle held high in the other. The current swept them sideways, the horse straining under the double load; for a moment it almost foundered, but the river was narrow here—he felt the pressure lessen against his upstream leg, and then they were in shallow water and the horse found its footing and they were climbing up the bank on the other side. When he figured they were far enough into the trees, he reined around and looked back.

He couldn't see them yet. He hoped that meant they couldn't see him, hadn't seen that dash across the river. He had no wish to stick around and find out. He passed the Winchester back for Ramona to return to its scabbard, then turned northeast and flicked the horse's flanks with his spurs.

In an hour they were deep up in timber to the north of the river, crossing narrow brushy ravines and little ridges that seemed to twist away in every direction. He figured the canyon was about four miles due south of them, across that river. Something in him was reluctant to turn that way, but if he aimed to get back in there it was better to do it soon, while Greene and his bunch were still out looking. Best would be to come at it along the top of that cliff on the east; thinking he was trying to get to town, Greene would likely have a man posted out on the flat to keep an eye on the road.

They were cutting south down a narrow little ridge when he reined abruptly to a halt, listening. He heard the sounds again, coming from the other side of the ridge: the clank of something metallic, and the stamp of hooves, like a staked horse straining to get loose from its tether.

Ramona's hands tightened on his waist. "You think it's one of them?" she whispered.

"Hard to say. They might have sent somebody across the river when they turned west through the pines. Pretty far up in this timber for a sentry to be watching for us, though. I'll check it out." He handed his Colt back to her and kicked a boot free to swing down out of the saddle. "You stay here. If you see somebody coming and it's not me, you better cut and run." Taking the Winchester, he started working his way up through the brush toward the spine of the ridge.

The slopes on this side of the river had seen a fire once; some of the tall pines still showed the scars, and scrub oak and fern had grown up beneath them. The underbrush was very thick, rising in some places far above his head. When he reached the top of the little ridge he could see nothing but more brush down the other side.

He looked back to see the horse standing where he had left it, halfway up the opposite slope of the ravine. Ramona had moved up into the saddle, bare legs dangling down free of the stirrups, holding the Colt awkwardly in both hands. Then he rose from his crouch, brushed aside a low-hanging oak limb, and started slowly down the ridge, stepping carefully to avoid the crackle of dry leaves underfoot.

Halfway down the slope, he heard that metallic clank again, and a brief scuffle of some sort, then silence again. He hunkered down against a tree trunk, but the sound was not repeated, and he could still see nothing but brush. Whatever it was, it was somewhere down to the left. He listened a minute or two longer. When he heard nothing else, he quietly levered a round into the chamber of the Winchester and started on, angling down to the left.

The brush seemed to thicken, becoming denser the farther down he got. He saw a patch ahead that looked virtually impenetrable, and it was a moment before he realized what it was: a slanted makeshift roof, dead branches thrown up over a sod dugout. That sudden scuffle came again, the clank of one metallic object against another, and now he saw movement down through the leafy limbs on the left—a patch of hide, a horse or a pack animal shifting about. Carefully he crept down to the back of the dugout and eased along to the left till he could see around the corner.

It wasn't a horse but a burro, tethered to a tree, a heavy pack lashed to its back. It was facing away from him, hooves planted wide apart, head lowered in the obstinate stance of its kind. Now it reared up against its tether, wrenching its neck, fighting itself half around, the clanking coming from a pair of shallow tin pans dangling from the pack. From the looks of the ground chewed up around the tree, it had been struggling to get loose for some time. Slocum scanned the terrain behind it, but there was no sign of a man. No sounds came from within the dugout. He lowered the Winchester and started toward the burro.

He saw the body before he'd taken two steps. It lay on flat ground in front of the dugout, on its back beside the burnt-out ashes of a campfire, arms out wide: an old man, gray-bearded, matted hair as long as a woman's. Slocum halted in mid-stride, the Winchester coming up, searching the trees around the site. When he was sure there was nobody else around, he went to kneel beside the body.

He could find no trace of a wound. The old man wore a long buckskin shirt belted around the waist, but there were no bullet holes in it and no sign of blood. He hadn't been dead long, no more than a few hours. Judging by the gray hair and the lines in the face, he had been on the far side of sixty; likely his heart had given out, overworked maybe from loading that burro one time too many. Likely he had been tramping these hills for years, looking for gold or for silver, for that fabled strike that kept old prospectors like him roaming the country. Didn't look like he'd ever found any. It was for sure he wouldn't be looking anymore.

Slocum left the body and stepped inside the dugout. Dim light, and not much else: a candle in a holder, a can of fat drippings, a rifle leaning in a corner. A sack of dried beans hung from the low rafters, along with several chunks of venison jerky. He yanked a chunk of jerky loose from its string and smelled it. Still good. Sudden saliva reminded him he hadn't eaten in quite a while.

He poured the beans out of the sack, filled it with as much of the venison as it would hold, then went out to strip the pack off the burro. A pickax, a shovel, a coffeepot, assorted items of a lonely man's life. There were two boxes of .44 ammunition for the rifle in the dugout but not much else of use. He went back to search the body, found a Bowie knife strapped to the old man's thigh and a pint of whiskey, miraculously unbroken, in a back pocket. He took the knife and the bottle and retrieved the rifle from the dugout. He hadn't found a pistol anywhere. For a moment he considered taking the old man's buckskin shirt—he was still bare-chested—but the thing looked to be carrying the sweat and grease of twenty years. The weather was warm; he could do without a shirt.

He removed the rope from around the burro's neck,

but with the pack gone, it took only a step or two and then just stood there twitching its tail. Probably couldn't get it to budge now if he wanted to, but it would forage for itself. He hated to leave the old man aboveground, but he had no time to bury a body. He could tell by the light filtering down through the trees that it was getting on toward late afternoon, and he wanted to get in and out of that canyon before nightfall caused Greene's bunch to give up the hunt. The knife strapped to his belt, the whiskey bottle in his pocket, carrying the sack of venison with both rifles and the boxes of shells, he started back up through the brush.

He couldn't find the horse when he topped the ridge. This was the spot he had seen it from last, just before slipping down to the dugout, but there was no sign of it now, and no sign of Ramona. He had been sure Greene's bunch had lost the trail; now he had a sudden image of them coming quietly out of the timber to take her while he was busy down below. He felt abruptly very exposed, standing there with two rifles and his hands too full to unlimber one in time if somebody was drawing down on him from inside those trees. But it wasn't far from the dugout to where he'd left her; he surely would have heard something if Greene's bunch had gotten anywhere close. Likely she had done the sensible thing and retreated back into the brush.

He decided to chance it; he called out her name and started down across the ravine.

He was almost on her before he saw her, back in the trees atop the opposite spine of the ravine. She had dismounted; now she led the horse out, her face pale, long bare legs showing scratches from the brush. The Colt looked heavy and awkward in her hand, but she had her finger on the trigger.

"Sorry I was gone so long," he said. "Found a dead man down there. An old prospector. You hear anything back the way we came?"

"Not so far." Her glance flicked from the rifles to his face. "Did somebody kill him?"

"He was an old man. His heart likely gave out on him. Here. I got us something to eat."

She relaxed then and took the sack of venison from him. He returned the Winchester to the saddle scabbard, then untied one end of the bedroll, worked the boxes of rifle shells up into it, and tied it tight again.

She was peering into the sack. "What is it?"

"Jerky. Dried meat. Not much, but it's better than nothing." He retrieved the Colt from her and stuck it in his waistband. "Take a piece, then we'll head back to the canyon. You'll have to carry this extra rifle. We may need it."

In the saddle again, he took a chunk of jerky to chew on, then tied the sack to the saddle horn. Ramona was already up behind him, one hand gripping his waist, the other holding the rifle. From the angle of the sun, he figured there were only three or four hours left till dark. Not much time. He touched spurs to the horse and reined off down toward the river.

16

They came down through sparse timber onto more level ground about twenty minutes later. The river came in sight after a few minutes more, wider here, stretching out into rocky shallows on either side. He halted just inside the tree line and scanned the river banks as far as he could see. No sign of Greene's bunch. Greene might have decided they had circled around and started for Bowie; if luck was with them, he would have taken his whole bunch toward town. On the other hand, he might have left somebody laying up just across that river.

"Give me that Winchester again. And hang on tight. That river may look shallow, but there's still a channel out there where the current's pretty fast."

"Do you think they're over there?"

"I doubt it. Just watch that current."

He figured there was a chance they were over there, but he didn't want her worrying about it. When he had the Winchester, he kneed the horse down out of the trees, Ramona holding tightly to his waist.

He kept his eyes on the far bank, ready to cut back toward the timber at the first sign of trouble. They were out on the grassy bank now, in sight of anybody watching. So far, so good. Then the horse started picking its way out through the rocky shallows, lurching and slipping on underwater rocks, and he had to give all his attention to the river.

The water was riding up his thighs when the horse suddenly plunged off an underwater ledge, going down head first. Slocum yanked up on the reins, rearing back in the saddle to keep from being thrown; and then they were in the swiftly running channel, the horse struggling to swim, the current sweeping it around till it was facing upstream and being carried rapidly downriver. He felt Ramona's hand begin to slip along his bare skin; she grabbed his belt, but he could tell by the sudden weight pulling him sideways that she was in trouble. He was trying to fight the horse toward the far bank and get a look at her at the same time. A backward glance showed him her frightened face, her body half off the horse; one leg had slipped down its right flank, the other riding up till she was half lying on its back, still trying to hold the rifle up out of the water. Only the clutch of her foot hooked over the horse's rump kept her from being swept away.

"Ditch the rifle," he shouted. "Ditch the rifle and grab on."

The horse struck an underwater rock, was spun sideways, and Slocum had to grab the saddle horn, fighting to stay in the saddle against the pull on his belt. Then her weight left him, he was sure she was gone, but a quick look showed her in the churning foam at his downstream leg, hanging on to the saddle strings, only her head above water, the current dragging her out almost horizontal, a flash of bare legs twisting behind her. Then the horse lurched under him, its front hooves clawing at the underwater ledge on the south side of the channel. He felt it swing around till its hind legs hit; for a moment it clawed frantically at the ledge, then heaved itself up into shallower water, dragging Ramona along after it. Slocum kicked his downstream boot clear of the stirrup and reached down to grab her by the wrist, pulling her up; she struggled briefly to right herself in the current, got a foot in the stirrup, and he hauled her back up behind him. Now the horse was leaping across the shallows toward the bank, slipping on a mossy rock, dodging others, and finally lunging up onto solid ground. Slocum let it trot on to the edge of the trees, then he reined it to a trembling halt, snorting, head tossing, its hide rippling off a little spray of water.

Ramona sagged against his back, both arms locked around his waist; he could feel her breasts swelling and subsiding as she fought to get her breath. He turned to see her pale face, her eyes concentrating on the need for air, her hair wet up to her ears.

"You all right?" he said.

She nodded, not looking at him, breathing heavily.

"We'll rest awhile," he said.

He swung a leg over the saddle horn, jumped down, and reached up to take her by the waist. She slid down against him and huddled in his arms, soaked to the skin, her nipples hard and erect from the cold water.

"You sure you're all right?" he said.

She nodded again. "Just give me some time. I think I swallowed too much water."

He led her to the shelter of a tree and sat her down on the grass, pulling the whiskey bottle from his back pocket. "Take a drink of this."

She took a drink, choked on it, coughed, and handed the bottle back. Then she huddled there, hugging her knees, the color slowly coming back to her face. He took a drink himself and returned the bottle to his pocket.

"Sorry I lost the rifle," she said.

"Not your fault. Don't worry about it. I saved the Winchester. And the Colt didn't get wet. We're all right." They were sitting in shade; the sun was already halfway down the western sky, and the sunlight filtering through the branches overhead had lost its force: she was beginning to shiver. "I'd suggest you take those things off and wring them out," he said. "Otherwise, you'll stay cold. We're going to be riding up through timber for quite a ways. Very little sunlight up there."

Her little smile revealed teeth on the verge of chattering. "You promise not to look?"

"You've gotten awful shy all of a sudden. You weren't so shy last night."

She blushed a little. "Last night's what made it different. I had a special time. I like you. That kind of makes me shy."

"No reason for it now. I can't promise not to look. Or even that I won't want to do more than look. But we ain't got time for that. It's getting late. I want to get that ransom before Greene's bunch gets back."

Still smiling a little, she got to her feet, turned her back to him, and slipped out of the pantalettes. The shirttails hung below her hips; he saw nothing bare except her legs. The pantalettes wrung out, she stepped back into them, then for some reason went down on her knees to take the shirt off. Having her back to him didn't do her much good; her breasts were just too large to be concealed by that slim torso. He saw both of them swelling out round and heavy as she reached back to strip the sleeves off her arms, watched them swing and jiggle as she wrung out the shirt. When she had it back on and buttoned up again, she turned to look at him, her smile broadening.

"Now how about you?" she said.

"I just got my legs wet. Besides, it's hard to wring out a pair of jeans."

"Coward."

He laughed and went to bring the horse.

Up behind him again, she slung her arms around his waist and murmured in his ear, "I'm sorry there wasn't time."

"So am I," he said, and kicked the horse up into the trees.

He figured they were about three miles north and a little ways east of the canyon. That was just about right; he wanted to skirt through the timber up on the east bluff, get close enough to see if there was a guard at the head of the trail leading in. If he was lucky, Greene wouldn't see any need for a guard, thinking he was gone for good, but he didn't know how Greene's mind worked. Greene might have reason to think Boldt would send somebody else out after him. Especially if Dooley had reported that run-in with Nolan and Walker.

He stayed alert as they climbed through the trees, listening for the sound of horses. He doubted if they were still searching this timber; the average man, thinking the ransom was gone, would concentrate all his riders on that flat country leading into town, where a single horse could be seen a mile away. Then again, a smarter man might leave a couple behind, just to cover his bets. And there was a chance that Greene was a smart man.

The sun was just touching the rim of the canyon when they came up through the trees toward the top of the bluff on the east. He had seen no sign of Greene's bunch on the way. The timber covered the east slope of the bluff, giving way at the top to a forty-yard expanse of flat, barren ground stretching across to the edge of the cliff. He would have liked a look down into the canyon, but anybody posted at the head of the trail would have a clear view of that flat ground, so he stayed in the trees, skirting the top of the bluff, till he judged they were near the south end. Then he reined to a halt, dismounted, and reached up to help Ramona down.

"You stay here," he said. "Keep the horse quiet. I'll go see if there's anybody guarding that trail."

Taking the Winchester, he left her with the horse and started up through the trees. When he neared the top of the slope, he dropped to his belly and crawled up to where he could see out over it.

He was almost directly even with the south end of the canyon; he recognized the terrain from having crossed it with Dooley and the other man when Dooley had taken him in to Red. A few tall pines grew right out to the edge of the cliff; he saw the tips of more of them flanking the trail as it dropped down away from the boulder that marked the head of it. The boulder was just visible in the shade of the trees, about a hundred yards away. That was where they'd left the guard on his way in. For a moment he could see only the boulder, then something moved just beyond it—a horse swinging its head up—and he saw a man hunkered down under a tree, wearing a beard and a Mexican poncho: Dooley.

Dooley was sitting in profile to him, in clear sight. Likely he could pick the man off from right here, but he couldn't risk it. If the rest of Green's bunch was anywhere close, the sound of a shot would bring them running. He would have to let Dooley see him, just long enough to let himself be recognized, then draw him down through the timber at a run. If he could get Dooley chasing him where the trees wouldn't allow a clear shot, he could maybe trick him up close enough to jump him and take him without gunplay. He turned and crept back down toward where he had left Ramona.

She was crouched down beside the horse, bare legs tucked up under her, hugging herself in the damp shirt. She looked frightened, but she didn't say anything as he came down beside her and took the reins.

"They've got a guard posted," he said. "I'm going to have to take care of him. Wait for me here."

"What if you don't come back?"

"I'll come back. Count on it. Just stick tight, and don't worry." He swung up into the saddle and started back up through the timber, keeping the Winchester out and ready just in case.

He skirted around to the left of where he had been lying a few minutes before; he wanted to put himself between Dooley and the south slope of the bluff. He couldn't risk staying in sight long enough to give Dooley a shot at him, and he would have to get down into those trees as quick as possible. If he remembered right, the timber gave out after only about a hundred yards, leaving only that barren rocky ground down toward the dry riverbed. There wouldn't be much room to maneuver.

He came up out of the timber at a walk, angling toward the south slope, toward where a man might pick up the trail down toward the riverbed and the road. He kept one eye on Dooley, the other on the trees, poised to dig in the spurs. For a moment he was afraid he was going to cross the open ground unnoticed; then he saw that movement again, Dooley's horse swinging its head up, sniffing the breeze, and its sudden high-pitched whinny brought Dooley to his feet, startled, looking Slocum's way.

Slocum kicked his own horse into a trot, restraining the impulse to lash it into a run. He saw Dooley reach for his Colt, halt suddenly as if realizing the range was too far for a handgun. Then Dooley wheeled and leaped for his horse, and Slocum dug in the spurs, plunging down into the timber.

He heard Dooley's horse start after him, breaking into a run almost immediately. The thick bed of pine needles underfoot muffled the sounds of his own horse; he crossed a stretch of rocky ground with a clatter, then there was the sudden silence of pine needles again, the horse skidding in the soft ground as it dodged tree trunks and large boulders thrusting up in its path. He chanced a look back for Dooley, couldn't see him yet; then he whipped through a stand of brush, springy branches thrashing at his legs, and he saw the start of the trail up ahead, curving around between two large boulders. He pulled in on the reins, wheeled the horse around behind the boulder on the left, kicked it in out of sight, and bent low in the saddle, listening.

Dooley wasn't very far back; he heard the muffled drumming of the horse coming down through the trees, then the clatter as it crossed that rocky ground and the sudden thrashing of the brush. When it sounded almost on him, just reaching the twin boulders, he spurred his own horse out onto the trail.

He hit Dooley just as the man came out from between the boulders. He yanked the reins around at the last minute, and the two horses slammed into each other, shoulder to shoulder; Dooley's horse squealed, wild-eyed, veering sideways toward the opposite boulder, and Slocum was swinging the Winchester around by the barrel end, the heavy stock catching Dooley right across the forehead.

Dooley was lifted right out of the stirrups. The spooked horse hit him with its rump as it bolted, sending him pinwheeling through the air; he hit the boulder headfirst and sprawled down to lie crumpled at the base of it. Slocum fought his own horse around, but Dooley didn't move. When he had brought it to a trembling standstill, he dismounted and knelt to take a look.

He didn't have to look close to see the man was dead. Only a little blood was trickling down into his eyes, but that Winchester had shattered bone; the skull was stove in from temple to temple above his eyebrows.

Slocum decided to leave him where he lay; it was better for the others to find him like this than to wonder where he was. With no bullet wounds to find, they would have no sure way of knowing what had happened. Dooley's horse had come to a halt forty yards off to the right of the trail, reins dangling; there was a chance they might think he'd been killed by a fall from the horse. And even if they surmised that Slocum had had a hand in it, they would figure it was in an attempt to break out to the road and town, not back into the canyon. And if Slocum was lucky, he would be in and out of there before they got back. He thrust the Winchester back into its scabbard, mounted up again, and turned the horse back up the slope.

He found Ramona where he'd left her, still crouching in the weeds at the base of a tree. She started when she heard the horse, white face peering around the tree trunk; then she recognized the horse and came up out of her crouch, looking very glad to see him.

He reined up beside her. "Told you I'd be back."

"Is he . . . Is it safe now?"

"So far. Now I got to get down into that canyon and sneak that ransom out. I figure you ought to lay low up here while I'm gone. No telling if I'll be able to climb back out of there before Greene's bunch shows up. Something happens to me, at least they won't get you."

"I'm going with you," she said. "I don't like being alone up here. It was bad enough just now. I don't think I could stand it with you gone any longer. And it's going to be dark soon."

"You sure? We might get trapped in there. Up here, at least you could head for the road, maybe intercept a stage or a wagon on its way to Bowie."

"Dressed like this?" She looked down at herself: big breasts lifting the shirt out and jiggling heavily every time she moved, so obviously bare under that thin cloth that even the nipples showed; long legs naked under the dangling shirttails. "I'd feel safer with you."

"You may have a point there. All right, let's give it a try." And he reached down to help her up.

17

The western rim of the canyon was silhouetted against a smoldering sky when they cleared the tree line and started across the flat ground. Likely you could still see the sun from down on the flat, but twilight would come pretty quick in that canyon. He was sure that dark would bring at least some of Greene's bunch back. This was cutting it very close.

The tops of the pines growing up the cliff face blocked the view into the canyon even after they started down the trail. He was struck by the sudden, unpleasant thought that maybe Greene and his men were already back, that maybe that was why Dooley had been posted up here. He could see no other reason for a guard. He could only hope that he was wrong, that Greene was just being cautious, like an animal wanting to make sure its burrow was safe to come back to. He watched for the first break in the trees, letting the horse pick its own way down the narrow rocky ledge, Ramona clinging to his waist.

Suddenly she said, "There's somebody down there."

The pines had begun to thin out; he could see the cabins now, halfway up the canyon, four on a side, facing each other, and the corral beyond the cabin where they had been tied together on the bunk. There were two horses in the corral and another, saddled, tied to the rail in front of the third cabin on the left. This wouldn't be as easy as he'd hoped, then. But at least the main bunch was still out hunting them somewhere.

"Can you still do it?" she said. "There's at least three of them."

"Three horses. I doubt if there's three men. One of those has to be Dory's horse. She wouldn't have ridden out hunting for us with the others. And likely one of them's for the Mexican woman. I figure there's one man down there, somebody to trade off guard shifts at the top of this trail. Let's just hope we get to the bottom of it before it comes time to change guards."

And before somebody chanced to look up this way and saw them riding in. He didn't mention that. From the way she was gripping his waist and watching the cabins, she had already thought of it herself. He curbed the impulse to pick up the pace a little; the only safe way to descend a trail like this was to give the horse its head. And if they were seen from one of those cabins, things were going to get very tricky—there was for sure no room to turn around.

He kept his eyes on the cabins all the way down, but if somebody had seen them, there was no sign of it. Then he felt Ramona's grip relax as they reached the bottom of the trail, and he spurred the horse into the strip of pines that bordered all four sides of the canyon. The trees put them out of sight; they climbed the little slope to the base of the cliff and turned north along it, Slocum keeping the horse at a trot on the soft bed of pine needles till he figured they were just about even with the first cabin. Then he reined to a halt, and they dismounted.

"I hid the money under that last cabin on the right," he said. "Opposite the one we were tied up in. I'll have to look things over before I can sneak it out, so this may take a while."

"What do you want me to do?"

"Just stay here. Stay out of sight and keep the horse quiet. I'll be back as soon as I can."

He left the Winchester with her, taking only his Colt, and worked his way down the slope till he reached the edge of the trees. Still nobody in sight around the cabins. That saddled horse was in front of the third one;

likely the man was in there. The Mexican woman was probably next door, where she lived with Greene. Unless she was cooking supper for the whole bunch, as she'd been doing that first night—that would put her in the first cabin, directly below him. He couldn't risk trying for the money till he knew where everybody was. And now was as good a time as any. He drew his Colt, took a deep breath, and dashed for the back of the first cabin.

He landed near the south corner and flattened himself up against the wall. The one window was just about at eye level, between him and the little porch. He eased carefully up to look inside.

He took the room in at a glance: fireplace, a few chairs, the table where he had sat with Red that first night. Somebody, likely the Mex woman, had repacked his war bag; it was stashed against the far wall. Otherwise, the cabin was empty. He skirted the porch, crept up to look around the opposite corner. No one in front. He set himself and dashed for the next cabin.

This was the one the Mexican woman shared with Greene, but he saw no one through the window. There was a table here, too, and a fireplace, and several sacks of something stacked near the front door. The door was standing open, but there was no sign of the woman out front, either. Then he saw movement just beyond the fireplace, and he realized he was looking through a side door into another room. He watched the woman cross to the front door and lay a blanket out to air on the porch railing. When he was sure she wasn't headed his way, he sneaked over to the window of the second room. A bedroom, empty except for the bed. He edged on along the wall till he could see up alongside the next cabin in line.

He couldn't see around to the front, but that was where that saddled horse had been tied to the rail. If there was a man here, that next cabin was where he would be. Luckily, there were no windows in the side wall. Slocum checked his Colt, then crept across the open ground to the back of the cabin.

He heard voices inside, a low murmur he couldn't make out, a man's voice, and then a woman, Dory, answering. Carefully, flattened against the wall, he eased up beside the window to where he could get a look inside.

He saw the man first—Sandy Quinn, standing bare to the waist, his back to the window; he looked to have just got his pants on and was buttoning them up. Quinn's shirt and gun belt were draped over the back of a chair; he moved to get the shirt, and now Slocum could see Dory on the bunk.

She was lying on her back, stark naked, one leg propped up on the mattress, hands idly stroking her breasts. She was grinning mischievously up at Quinn, saying something to him, arching her back, teasing him. She was a sight to behold even in the dim light of the room, that voluptuous blond body laid out naked like that; Slocum didn't have to ask himself what Quinn had been doing with his spare time between guard shifts. Dory lifted one little foot to prod Quinn in the thigh, but Quinn just gave her a pat on the leg, and she laughed and rolled off the bunk to reach for her clothes. Slocum ducked down beneath the window and light-footed it up to the last cabin in the row.

He doubted there was anybody in this one. The windows were boarded up, and it hadn't looked in use when he'd been in there. Besides, he was sure Quinn was the only one of Greene's men left in the canyon. Ramona's dress and his own shirt still lay in the dust behind the back porch, where they had been dropped the day before. He stepped over them, made his way around to the front corner of the cabin, and looked back down the row.

What he saw brought him back around the corner fast, swearing to himself. Quinn had come out on the porch and was leaning on the railing, rolling up a smoke. He was fully dressed now, his gun belt strapped on, and he was facing this way.

Slocum checked the skyline to the west, wishing Dory had succeeded in coaxing Quinn back down on that bunk. He figured there was about an hour of real light left. If Quinn didn't go back inside soon, he would have to try and take him. He couldn't afford to wait for the cover of dark, not with the others likely due back anytime. Even as that thought came to him, he heard the sound of horses coming up toward the cabins from the south.

It was Greene, leading the rest of the bunch at a trot. Slocum counted four, five, six riders. Figure one man left at the head of the trail; that made eight in all, counting Quinn. He was trapped in this canyon now for sure, but he figured he was lucky to have gotten in at all. A few minutes more, and he would have encountered the whole bunch of them up on top of that bluff. He hadn't seen them coming down the trail, but they couldn't have been far behind. They had found Dooley; he could see the body draped over Dooley's horse. But they didn't suspect he was here; if they did, they would be coming in alert, looking for him, not straggling up to the first cabin the way they were.

He saw Greene dismount and disappear into the cabin. The Mex woman came out of the second cabin and headed that way. Greene wouldn't be happy with the turn of events, and that would put the others on edge. No chance to get to the ransom now. He would have to hole up, wait till dark, hope to sneak out when they were all asleep. Assuming he and Ramona weren't discovered before then. There would be no tying them together on a bunk this time. This time they would beat him till he broke. Or until he died. And they would insist he lead them to the ransom himself. And likely they'd kill him as soon as they got it.

The others had swung down out of the saddle. Now a couple of them started leading the horses his way, up toward the corral. He went back along the wall, checked to make sure there was nobody in sight behind the cabins, then sprinted up the slope. Up in the pines, he crouched behind a tree trunk and scanned the row of cabins. When he was sure he hadn't been seen, he set out at a trot back toward the bottom of the trail.

Ramona had led the horse down away from the cliff into the denser shelter of the pines. She was pale and big-eyed, and she looked dismayed to see him empty-handed.

"You didn't get it?"

"I couldn't get to it. They came back too soon. Come on, we're going to have to hole up till after dark. Let's get into that mine shaft."

"Can we get out after dark?"

"We'll have to try. There's sure to be a guard on the trail, but I can maybe take him by surprise if I climb the last half of it on foot. It's the only chance we've got."

He was ten yards ahead of Ramona, leading the horse, when they reached the open ground where the narrow rails emerged out of the mine. He halted the horse just inside the trees and surveyed the terrain below. Most of the men had disappeared, but he couldn't tell which cabins they had gone to. The horses had been unsaddled; the two men who had led them up to the corral were just closing the gate on them.

He felt something brush his arm: Ramona crouching down beside him. "We're going to have to make a dash for the mine," he said. "Soon as I say 'go,' you run. I'll be right behind you."

He drew the Winchester out of its scabbard, watching the two men straggling back from the corral. With no light in the cabin windows, it was impossible to tell if there was anybody looking this way. When the two men disappeared from sight in front of the cabin directly down from the mine, he tapped Ramona on the shoulder.

"Go."

He caught a flash of bare legs as she ran for the mine, but he was watching the cabins. He waited a minute, then two. A quick glance told him she'd made it inside the shaft. No reaction from below. He waited a minute more, then rose to his feet and ran after her, the clatter of the horse sounding very loud along the rocky ground.

He had to grab it by the bridle and pull its head down to get it into the mine—the shaft had been built to accommodate burros. It balked at first, slipping and knocking up against the little trolley rails, but he heaved on the bridle and dragged it in till he was sure it was out of sight. Then he worked his way back along its flank, stroking its hide and talking soothingly, trying to calm it down while he got a look at what little he could see of the cabins.

A lamp had been lit in the first cabin, the one Greene had gone into. He caught a glimpse of the Mexican woman silhouetted briefly against the window, then two or three other figures moving around in there. The two men coming back from the corral had crossed up to the third cabin on the other side; he watched them mount the porch and waited till a lamp flickered alight in there. No sign of anybody else. And no sign that anybody had been looking during that dash from the trees to the mine. The horse was settling down but was still nervous, shifting from hoof to hoof, trying awkwardly to raise its head against the low ceiling. He returned the Winchester to its scabbard, edged back up to seize the bridle again, and led the horse deeper into the mine.

There was just enough light coming in from outside to see by. He coaxed the horse around the first bend in the shaft, into the first wide chamber, where Ramona had been kept chained up The ceiling was higher here, high enough for the horse to stand upright. Ramona was huddled on the wooden storage chests against the left wall, across the chamber from those four copper kegs he remembered from the first night.

"What now?" she said.

"First I want to see what's going on down there. Then we wait for dark."

He checked to see the horse was settled down, then made his way back to the mouth of the mine.

18

More lights were showing now. Somebody had lit a lamp in the first cabin in the opposite row, up from where Greene was, and the window glowed in the cabin where he'd seen Dory and Quinn. That made four cabins occupied at the moment, unless somebody was doing without light. There was maybe a half hour left till dark; all the terrain down there was still visible. One man was strolling down between the two rows of cabins, and vague figures were moving around behind a window here and there, but he couldn't see anybody else.

There had been two horses in the corral when he and Ramona had ridden in; there were seven in there now. He had counted six riders; one of them, probably Greene, had kept a horse down at his cabin. Two horses ready to ride, Quinn's and Greene's, and Quinn's was saddled only because he'd been scheduled to go on guard. They weren't likely to head out again tonight, then. He wondered if they had given up.

For the first time it occurred to him that Greene might have sent a man into Bowie, to see if he and Ramona had made it to town. That would take a while— unless Greene had sent a man as soon as he'd found them gone that morning. A man leaving the canyon that morning could make it back here within the next hour or two. Then they might start putting things together: Boldt's saddlebags on his horse even after he was in the canyon; bedding down close by instead of heading for town; the death of Dooley less than two hours ago. A smart man could read the truth out of that. And if they decided he'd hidden the money in the canyon and come back in after it, somebody might just think of this mine as the logical place for him to be.

He couldn't afford to be caught like this. The odds were stacked too high against him. He turned and went back into the chamber where he'd left Ramona.

The light was getting very dim this far back in the shaft. The horse was standing patiently in the center of the chamber, reins dangling. Ramona was sitting on the storage chests, the blankets tucked up around her legs.

"Be dark soon," he said. "They look to be settling in down there, but I don't want to take any chances. Look and see what's in those storage chests."

He crossed to the copper kegs against the opposite wall and tapped one of them on the side. Sounded like it was full. He worked the top off it and scooped out a palmful of the contents, smelled it, tasted it. Black powder, all right. And still potent. He forced the top back on and tapped each of the other three. All full.

Ramona had the lid of a storage chest open. "Looks like mining things. Fuses and stuff."

"How much fuse?"

"Lots of it."

"Good. Bring all you can up to the front. And bring that lantern, too."

One by one, he rolled the kegs along the trolley rails and set them upright against the wall at the mouth of the shaft. Then he took the canteen off the horse and the boxes of extra ammunition and carried them back as well. Ramona had brought the lantern and the fuse, an armful of it, coiled up like a rope. He gave her a drink, took one himself, then upended the canteen and let the water gurgle out.

"What are you going to do?" she said.

"Going to set up a little diversion out there, just in case things get hot. We won't need this. There's still that bucket of water they had for you back there."

When the canteen was empty, he worked the top off

one of the kegs, scooped up a handful of black powder, and started funneling it down into the canteen. After every few handfuls, he dropped several cartridges down into the powder, till he had emptied half a box. When the canteen was full, he emptied the whiskey out of the bottle he had got off the old prospector and did the same with it.

"Do you want the lantern?" she said.

"Don't need it yet. But keep it close by here where I can find it in the dark."

He put the top of the keg back on, took the knife, and placed the tip of it straight down on the lid. Then, using one hand like a hammer, he pounded on the butt of the knife till he'd driven the tip of it through the thin copper, creating a small slit. No way to treat a good blade, but for what he had in mind, he didn't need a sharp knife. Hard to estimate the burning time of fuse that had been sitting for a while, too, but he measured out a length that looked right, cut it off, and forced one end of it down through the slit and into the black powder in the keg. Then he measured off equal lengths of fuse and did the same thing with the other kegs.

"Let's hope we don't have to use these, but if we do, at least we got something to even the odds."

Full dark had set in now; a half moon was just lifting up over the eastern rim of the canyon. He could have done without the moon, but he couldn't help that. He could see no change down around the cabins. He took the rest of the fuse from Ramona—a couple hundred feet of it at least.

"Stay here," he said. "I'll be back in a minute."

Carrying the canteen and the whiskey bottle, the fuse tucked under his other arm, he left the shaft and set out along the base of the cliff on the right. He figured he had enough fuse to cover that open ground. When he reached the edge of the pines, he turned down along the tree line till he'd gone about twenty yards. Then he laid everything on the ground and started digging a hole with the knife.

He decided to use the whiskey bottle here; he wouldn't need too big a hole. When he had it dug, he put the whiskey bottle in and started tamping the earth down around it, leaving only the neck aboveground. He forced an end of the fuse through the neck, as far down into the powder as he could make it go. Not much in the way of artillery, but it would make noise, anyway. And in a night battle, that might create enough confusion to be useful.

He checked the lamplit windows down at the bottom of the slope. Still no change. He got to his feet and started backing toward the mine, carrying the canteen, paying out fuse as he went.

Ramona was crouched just inside the entrance, her face pale in the moonlight. He ran the fuse about eight or ten yards inside, then cut it off with the knife.

"See anything suspicious?"

"Nothing," she said. "Are you finished?"

"Not yet. I'm setting charges out on both sides of us. Might create confusion if we have to get out of here in a hurry." He was returning the knife to his belt when a sudden thought brought him up short. "I haven't got any matches. They were in my shirt. Did you see any in that bedroll?"

"There were some where they had me chained up. They left them so I could light that lantern when I wanted. I'll see if they're still there."

While she crept back into the mine, he hunkered down at the entrance, watching the cabins. Light still showed in four of them, one of them right next to the one where he'd hidden the ransom. Might be very tricky getting to the money with men so close by. And without matches, all this stuff would do him no good at all.

He heard a noise behind him and turned to see Ramona

emerging into what little moonlight there was near the mouth of the shaft.

"I found them," she said. "There's only about ten of them left."

"That's enough. That's all we need. You keep them. And stay close to this entrance. I'm going to go set this other charge."

He slipped out of the shaft and worked his way along the base of the cliff till he reached the pines on the left. Not as close as on the other side, but he figured he had enough fuse. Down in the trees, about even with where he had buried the bottle, he put the canteen and the coiled fuse down and started digging with the knife. Rocky ground here, and he needed a bigger hole; it took him a good deal longer to get it dug. The scrape of the knife sounded awfully loud, but that was just his imagination. The noise wouldn't carry down to those cabins. Once he thought he heard something from back near the mine, but that was likely imagination too—he couldn't see anything unusual along the slope. When he figured the hole was big enough, he laid the canteen in it and filled it up again, leaving just the opening in the top of the canteen free. Then he packed the earth down tight and thrust in the fuse, the way he had done with the bottle.

He was just about to start back toward the mine when he heard the slap of a door shutting down at the bottom of the slope. The lamp had gone out in the cabin next to where he'd hidden the money. In the dim glow of light from the moon and the other lit windows, he saw two men descending the porch, starting down toward the cabin Greene was in. Now the first cabin in the far row went dark too. There looked to be more men moving around in Greene's cabin; they all seemed to be gathering in there. Supper, maybe. That was good. If he timed it right, he could get to that money while they were all occupied. Paying out the last of the fuse behind him, he climbed back up the slope to the entrance of the mine.

Ramona wasn't there.

He paused just inside the shaft, searching the darkness. No sign of her anywhere. He dropped the end of the fuse and edged along the wall, his leg brushing a copper keg. Still no sign of her. She could be farther back in the shaft, but he had distinctly told her to stay near the entrance. His boot struck something small and light and sent it rattling a foot or two along the ground. He bent to pick it up: the box of matches. He had told her to keep those, too; she would have no reason to drop them here, where they might be hard to find in the dark. He remembered that sound he'd heard while burying the canteen, but surely he would have heard more if somebody had got to her here.

He drew his Colt and took another step along the shaft. "Ramona?"

The voice that answered was not Ramona's but Dory's.

"Don't come any closer, Johnny."

19

He froze in mid-stride, one hand braced against the wall, the Colt in the other. He couldn't see her, couldn't see anything but darkness. He heard something move back where the shaft widened out into the chamber, but that was the horse, stirring restlessly. If he judged it right, she was between him and the horse, and she had to have a gun. What he wanted to know now was whether she had come up here on her own hook, or whether she had a man or two with her. And what she had done with Ramona.

"Ramona?"

"She's got a shotgun on me," Ramona said. "I didn't see her coming, but she's alone."

"Shut up," Dory said. "If you want to live, you'll do what I say."

A smart woman, Ramona—smart enough to tell him what he needed to know. And now he had a sense of where they were; the voices had come from somewhere near the first bend in the shaft, just where it opened out into the chamber. Likely Dory would have Ramona in front of her, using her as a shield. He couldn't risk a shot for fear of hitting Ramona. And even if he missed her, he might hit the horse; he needed that horse. He couldn't feature killing a woman, anyway, especially Dory, a woman he'd known and once thought of as a friend, somebody once closer than a friend. But it might come to that. A man could do a lot of things if he really had to.

"Don't try anything, Johnny," Dory said. "I can tell you're thinking on it, but don't. You can't see me, but

153

there's moonlight at your back. You try anything, and I'll kill her.''

"I knew you had a lot of things in you, Dory, but I didn't know you had it in you to kill.''

"You've killed to get what you wanted. So has Red. And all those other men down there. Who's to say a woman shouldn't kill to get what she wants?''

He was hoping his eyes would adjust to this deeper darkness, enough at least to let him see movement, maybe enough to where he could see the outline of her. Not likely if she was still wearing that black blouse and the dark skirt. But maybe moonlight on her face, or on Ramona's bare legs, if he could get her to come out a little ways. If he got close enough, there might be a chance to tackle her, get that shotgun away before she could fire. He had to keep her talking.

"How did you know we were up here?''

"First place I thought to look. When Ashe came back and said you'd led them on a goose chase today, I knew you didn't have the money with you. And if you didn't have it, it had to be in this canyon. Ashe hasn't figured that out yet, but Ashe is mad, and Ashe don't think too good when he's mad. So I'll just take it all for myself. Tell me where it is Johnny.''

"I haven't got it. You think I'd still be here if I did?''

"I didn't say you had it. I said tell me where it is. You can't win, but I will no matter what happens. I can turn you over to Ashe, and I'll still get a cut, but Ashe'll probably have you killed. Maybe Ramona, too. You tell me where the money is, then I won't have to share it, and you can get out of here alive. You've got no choice, Johnny. You try to stop me, and I'll kill Ramona right here. You know I got good reason to, even without the money. And I got nothing to lose, now Sam has kicked me out. I need that money. I'm getting too old to start over at the bottom in my business.''

"You fire that shotgun, Dory, and I'll see the blast. I'll have a bullet in you before you can get off another."

"A lot of good it'll do you. Ramona'll be dead, and you wouldn't live another ten minutes. One shot would bring half a dozen men up here. I told you, you can't win. You have to do what I want. That way everybody gets something. I get the money; you get to live—you and Ramona."

He still couldn't see anything. It was just too dark in there. He wondered if she really could see him, if there really was that much moonlight at his back. It was possible she had lied about that, that she knew where he was from the sounds he'd made, from when he'd called out to Ramona. If she was bluffing, he could maybe get a little closer to her. He had to try something, because she was right: He didn't have many options. He hefted the Colt and took another step into the shaft.

"Don't move, Johnny. Don't move, or I'll have to do it."

He froze again, feeling his belly suck up against his ribs, expecting the sudden blast of the shotgun. There was fear in her voice, the fear of somebody on the edge of cracking, afraid of what she had determined to do. He couldn't risk testing her again.

"All right. All right, you win."

"Tell me where the money is, Johnny. Quick."

"It's under the porch of the cabin down there. Opposite the cabin you kept me in. I stashed it under there in a canvas sack."

She was silent for a bit, as if trying to judge whether that was true, and figuring out a way to check it. Then: "That wouldn't be another lie, would it? Like the one you told Ashe?"

"It's no lie, Dory."

"We'll see," she said. "Because what we're going to do now, I'm going to bring Ramona out toward you. You're going to tie her up and gag her, and then you and me, we'll go look under that porch. Everybody's in the first cabin—we can get down there without being seen. If the money's there, you can come back up here and free Ramona. But not before you've helped me get out with the money. Is that agreed?''

"Whatever you say."

"Good. Now throw your gun toward me. Throw it all the way over where I am.''

Cautiously, Slocum reversed the Colt and pitched it into the dark. He heard it land with a metallic clatter just short of where he judged Dory to be.

"Now back away," Dory said. "Back up slow till you're right at the entrance. I'm coming out. And don't try anything unless you want this shotgun to go off.''

He backed slowly away, keeping one hand on the wall to guide himself. His other hand was on the knife in his belt. She didn't know he had the knife; that was an advantage he still had. Thinking she had him disarmed, she might relax a little now, get a little careless with that shotgun. If she got out here where he could see her in the moonlight, there might still be a chance to take her. His skin crawled at the thought of sinking a knife into that supple little body, remembering the times he'd held it up close against his own, naked and warm and writhing with the pleasure they'd been making together. But maybe he wouldn't have to. If he could get close enough to use the knife, he could maybe overpower her before she had time to react.

He heard her edging toward him, the slow cautious slide of her feet along the floor of the shaft till she struck the Colt, silence as she bent to pick it up.

Then a sudden scuffle: a hand striking flesh; a foot knocking the Colt away; gasps; a little cry from Dory; Ramona's frightened shout: "Slocum?" He launched himself into the dark as the shotgun clattered to the ground, heard a thud against the wall, a tearing of cloth, frantic gasps as they fought. Somebody lurched into him, was yanked away; then they both went down, and he dived onto them, took an elbow in the ribs, felt a squirming back under his hand but couldn't tell whose. He touched a bare leg and realized it was Ramona just as she rolled away, kicking and gasping: "Help me. I've got her by the arms. Help me!"

He rolled toward them, came up against Dory fighting to free her arms from behind her back; she tried to knee him in the groin, but he blocked it, grabbed her by the hair and got a hand across her mouth just in time to stifle a scream. She bit him then, still kicking, and he wrenched his hand loose and clipped her hard on the chin, and she went suddenly slack.

He lay there for a moment, breathing hard, still dazed by the suddenness of it. He still had her by the hair, but he could tell she was out cold by the way she sagged against him. Ramona was trying to catch her breath; she was only an arm's length away, but he couldn't see her in the dark. He released his grip and got to his feet.

"That took nerve," he said. "You did a good job."

"I felt the shotgun leave my back when she bent over. I thought I could knock her down, but she fought pretty hard. But I'm bigger than she is."

"Find that shotgun. I'll get something to tie her up with."

The horse was a little spooked. He had to sweet-talk it to get close, reaching blindly out till he found its rump, then feeling his way up its side to the rope coiled from the saddle horn. He cut two lengths of rope and made his way back along the wall, unable to see a thing.

"Over here," Ramona said. "Be careful. I've got the shotgun, but your Colt is still lying there somewhere."

He edged out from the wall, feeling with his boots till he encountered Dory, then knelt down and started tying her wrists behind her back. He bound her ankles together and tied them up tight to her wrists. Uncomfortable, maybe, but she wouldn't feel it for a while. And he didn't want her getting loose.

"You got something to gag her with?"

"She tore a sleeve off this shirt," Ramona said. "You might as well use that."

When he had the gag on tight, he felt around on the ground till he found his Colt. All he could see was the faint oval of moonlight that was the mouth of the mine. It seemed like an hour since he'd come in from outside, since he'd had a look at those cabins, and he didn't like the feeling. Sooner or later somebody else was going to draw the same conclusion Dory had. The best he could hope for would be to see it coming. That would put them under siege in this mine, but at least they could defend themselves. Another story if he didn't see it coming. They could survive Dory catching them unawares; surviving a surprise attack by half a dozen men wouldn't be so easy.

He sensed Ramona somewhere in the dark beside him. "You all right now?"

"I'm all right," she said. "I'm scared, but I'm all right. I want to get out of here."

"Soon as we can. You watch Dory. I'll go see how things look down at the cabins."

He tucked the Colt in his waistband and started for that oval of moonlight.

20

Back at the entrance, he searched around on the ground till he found the ends of the fuses he'd run into the shaft from the charges. He had pocketed the matches; now he wrapped the fuse ends around one of the black-powder kegs, where he could get at them fast.

Lamps were lit in only two of the cabins now, Dory's and the first one, where Greene was. Dory had said everybody was in that first cabin; from what he could see through the window, he figured she was telling the truth. They looked to be holding some kind of powwow down there; he would have given a lot to know what was being said. And he hoped nobody started wondering where Dory was.

Ramona crept up beside him, carrying the shotgun. "Dory's still out," she said. "How do things look?"

"They're all in that first cabin. I think I can get to the money now. Wait for me here. Be careful with that shotgun. If you see somebody coming, it may be me. I'll call out when I'm close enough."

He left the mine and started stealthily down the slope, aiming for the shelter of the pines on the left.

He descended through the trees at an easy lope, his boots quiet on the thick pine needles, the night air cool and sharp after the close quarters of the mine. Moonlight filtered down through the branches; the sky was clear overhead, glittering with stars. He felt a sudden inexplicable exhilaration, the urgency of pressing time—with luck, they could be starting up that trail in another twenty minutes. And he would be very glad to put this canyon behind him.

He halted at the edge of the trees, crouching to present a smaller silhouette, and checked the ground below the tree line. The cabin he'd been tied up in lay almost directly below him. There was nobody in sight. He drew his Colt and dashed out across that open ground.

It wasn't till he had reached the cabin that he heard the sounds coming from the corral. He flattened himself against the back wall, just inside the north corner. He could see nothing up there but horses, one of them drifting along the rail as if bored by the spot it had been standing in, but there was definitely somebody within earshot. What he'd heard was a man swearing as if to himself, and the clatter and slap of a saddle being thrown onto a horse's back. Whoever it was was blocked from sight by the corner of the cabin, but that didn't mean he hadn't been seen on that run from the trees. He sidestepped to the corner and looked around.

The line of sight put two sides of the corral between him and the other man. He could see the dark shape of a horse and vague movements somewhere just outside the gate. He didn't think he had been seen; the man looked to be tightening up the saddle cinch. Only one man, and one horse being saddled. Slocum hoped he was riding out for good. That would be one less he would have to worry about. Now the man swung up into the saddle and started down toward the cabins.

Slocum ducked back, lowered himself to his belly, and eased his head around the corner again. The man was slumped in the saddle, hat pulled low—not somebody he recognized. When the horse passed the far corner, disappearing along the front of the cabin, Slocum rose to his feet and proceeded along the side wall to watch it continue on down past the others, heading at an unhurried walk toward the south end of the canyon. Likely going up to relieve the guard at the top of the trail. It wasn't Quinn, though; he would have recognized Quinn.

Likely Quinn had been taken off the guard roster after trading shifts with Dooley all day.

Slocum searched the dark along the cabin fronts. Still two saddled horses tied to the hitching rails: Greene's, in front of the first cabin, and Quinn's, in front of the third. And those were still the only two cabins showing light, too far away to give him any trouble here. The porch where he'd stashed the ransom was directly opposite him, a twenty- or thirty-yard run at most. The rider heading for the south trail had receded into the dark; there was nobody else in sight. He launched himself away from the wall and darted across the open ground toward that porch.

He hit the ground beside it, crouched down to where he could just see across the steps toward the rest of the cabins. No sign of reaction from down there. When he was sure it was safe, he ducked under the porch and felt around in the weeds for the canvas sack.

He found it up under the far side, dragged it out, and opened the drawstring to look inside. The money was still there. He felt that brief flare of exhilaration again—not much longer now. Checking the lighted windows down the row, he sprinted back across the open ground to the opposite cabin.

He moved fast now, in a hurry to get back to the mine and out of here. He located Ramona's dress in the dust at the back of the cabin and scooped it up; his shirt was shredded and useless, but she couldn't enter town half-naked like she was; she would want what was left of that dress. He tucked his Colt into his waistband and, carrying the dress and the money sack, headed back up into the trees to the right of the mine.

He was only about ten yards into the trees when he heard what sounded like footsteps, just behind him and to the left. He dropped the money sack and wheeled, going for his Colt, but he was too late. He saw the dark blur of a man springing from behind a tree, and then something hit him hard on the head, and he went down.

He didn't go all the way out. He caught himself on hands and knees, stunned, trying to hold on to consciousness, but he couldn't make it. Strength drained from him like water, and he felt himself sag to the ground, his face in the pine needles, an overwhelming pain reverberating through his head like an echo. Then the reverberations began to fade; he felt somebody turn him over on his back and the Colt was lifted from his waistband.

A voice said, "Sorry, Cap'n, but I had to do it."

His head had begun to clear; he saw Red standing over him, carrying a Winchester, the money sack already tied to his belt. The barrel of that Winchester was evidently what he'd been hit with. Slocum rose to a sitting position and put his head in his hands, that dull throb still reverberating through his skull.

"So you had it hid in here all the time," Red said. "I should have thought of that. I didn't hurt you bad, did I?"

"I ain't dead, if that's what you mean. Where'd you come from?"

"Come out looking for Dory. They're having a sort of meeting down there, and I ain't too popular right now. Been some harsh talk against me for letting you in here. Figured if I stayed, it might come to a point where I'd have to call somebody out just to save my pride. So I thought I'd go talk to Dory, only she wasn't in her cabin. Started up here looking for her when I saw you down around the cabins."

"And you had to club me."

"We ain't exactly on the same side, Cap'n. Or have you forgot?"

"You just reminded me pretty good."

Slocum rolled over and tried to get to his feet, but a sudden wave of dizziness brought him down on his hands and knees again. When the dizziness passed, he saw that Red had backed up a bit and was training the Winchester on him.

"Don't try nothing funny, Cap'n. I might can still consider you a friend, but I'll kill you if I have to. And don't count on that Warren woman, either. I got close enough to the mine to see she has a gun. I heard the horse back in there, too. That's my horse you took. I figure I'll take it and ride out. I can talk my way past the guard."

"I'll have to follow you, Red. You know that."

"Maybe. If you get out of here, you're welcome to try. Right now I got other things to worry about. Now come on. I want to get to that mine. I'll have this rifle in your back, so when we get close, you sing out to that Warren woman and have her throw that gun out."

Slocum's head still ached, but the ringing had gone away, and he could feel his strength coming back. He got to his feet, one eye on the cabins, the other on Red. Sooner or later, that bunch down there was going to break up. He couldn't tell what Red might do; if Red drew their attention up here, the fat would be in the fire, and he didn't even have a gun to defend himself with. He bent to pick up Ramona's dress, thinking he could maybe throw it in Red's face and dive for his legs before he could untangle himself.

"Leave it lay," Red said. "Just head on up through the trees. We're going to come at her from the side, where she can't see us."

Slocum had the dress in his hand, but he could tell Red knew what he was thinking. He couldn't risk it. He dropped the dress and started up through the trees.

When they reached the cliff face, Red turned him left along it, staying a yard or two behind him. Slocum took it slow, less to delay things than because he wanted to keep a fix on where Red was; he had hoped the muzzle of that rifle might stay right against his back, where he could maybe wheel and wrench it loose, but Red was too smart for that. By the time they reached the break in the trees, Slocum had given up on the idea; he would just have to play this out and see if another chance came along later.

He halted at the edge of the trees. Moonlight bathed the open ground in front of the mine, gleaming on what iron still showed through the rust on the trolley rails running down toward the cabins. He figured nobody from inside that first cabin could see him, but if there was anybody out away from the lamplight and looking this way, they might see any movement up here.

"Ease on out there," Red whispered. "Call out to her when you're close enough. You know what to say."

Slocum started out into the moonlight, one hand on the cliff face to guide himself, stepping slow and careful to keep things quiet. Alone in the dark like that, her imagination likely playing tricks on her, even small night sounds might make her nervous, and he didn't want her spooked before he got close enough to identify himself. She'd been through a lot in the last few hours, and she was sure to be scared, and she had that shotgun.

He stopped again about ten feet from the mine entrance, listening. Red's breathing sounded awfully loud behind him, but he couldn't hear anything from her. The rails running out of the shaft were clearly visible, but she was too far inside to see.

"Ramona? Ramona, It's Slocum. Stay where you are. Don't move till you hear me out. There's a man out here with a gun in my back. It's Red Wylie. He wants the money and the horse, but if we do what he wants he won't harm us. You'll have to throw that shotgun out and come out of there, but you'll be all right. You can take my word on that, but you have to do it now."

There was no reaction from the mine. Slocum tensed, listening, a rifle at his back, an inexperienced woman with a shotgun no more than ten feet in front of him. Inexperienced and scared.

"Ramona? We have no choice. Throw the shotgun out where he can see it."

Still nothing but silence. He could picture her in there, scared, confused, her frightened mind trying to assimilate this abrupt and unexpected announcement out of the dark, trying to decide what to do. She was capable of acting on her own; she had proved that when she tackled Dory. He only hoped she realized this wasn't the time for it.

He was about to call out again when a sudden sound came from the mine, and Ramona wheeled out around the corner of the entrance, the shotgun up and pointing right at him.

He shrank to a sudden half crouch, feeling his belly cramp up toward his rib cage, every muscle trying to shrink out of the way of that shotgun.

She didn't fire, but she didn't move, either.

"You can't hit him," he said, talking softly, trying by the sound of his voice to keep her calm. "It's no use. Go ahead and put the shotgun down. We'll be all right. Red's cutting out on his own hook. He won't tell the rest of them we're here."

Behind him, Red said, "All I want's the money and the horse. Do as he says."

She brought the shotgun down a bit, but it was still aiming at him. Her bare legs were bright in the moonlight, but he couldn't see the expression on her face.

"It's all right," he said. "Put the shotgun down."

Slowly then, she lowered the shotgun and laid it on the ground at her feet.

"Now back away," Red said. "Back over to the other side of the shaft. And do it slow. I never shot a woman before, but no woman ever pointed a shotgun at me, either."

When Ramona had backed away, Red skirted around

to where the shotgun was and, keeping the rifle trained on Slocum, bent to pick it up. He transferred the rifle to the crook of his arm, swung the shotgun around toward Slocum, and jerked his head at Ramona.

"Now go in there and lead that horse out. I know there's a rifle in the scabbard. Just leave it in there. Remember, any trouble up here will just bring the rest of them running. Just do like you're told, and you got nothing to fear from me."

Ramona looked to Slocum. "Will he do what he says?"

"He'll do what he says. Don't try anything. Just give him the horse and let him ride out. We'll decide what to do after that."

She hesitated, glanced at the shotgun, then crept back into the shaft.

Slocum watched the cabins down below. He had already decided there was nothing he could do to stop Red, that the best thing was to just let him go. He couldn't risk anything here in the canyon; when Red was gone, he could probably sneak a horse or two out of that corral and set out after him. The man he'd seen riding out had probably relieved the guard by now; he figured there was only one, and the first one would already be on his way back in. He could lay low till the man had corraled his horse, and then make his move. If Red talked his way past the new guard, that would leave seven men he had to deal with in case something went wrong, six of them in the canyon. Pretty long odds. To have a chance at all, he would have to talk Red into leaving him at least one gun.

Ramona came out of the shaft now, leading the horse by the bridle. The horse snorted and swung its head up, glad to be free of that low ceiling. Slocum checked the lamplit cabin down below. No sign of trouble yet. But now he heard sounds from within the mine, high-pitched nasal whimpers: Dory trying to cry out through her gag.

"What's that?" Red swung the shotgun toward Ramona. "Is that Dory?"

Ramona didn't answer.

"Is that Dory, Cap'n? You got Dory in there?"

"Take the horse and ride out, Red. You got the money. You'll have a hard enough time getting away from here as it is."

"You let me worry about that. What did you do to her?"

"Nothing. She came up here and tried the same thing you did. She's tied up in there. You'd best leave her be. I'll see no harm comes to her."

Red jerked his head at Ramona again. "Go bring her out." When Ramona had disappeared into the shaft, he swung back toward Slocum. "You better hope she ain't hurt."

"I had to knock her out, but she's all right. But taking her with you ain't a smart thing, Red. You know that."

"What I do about Dory's my business," Red said. "That's the one thing in my life I can stand by—I've always been there when Dory's needed me. You can call me a fool for it, like you already done, but you don't know the way it is. You don't know Dory like I do. There's times she really needs me, times she's glad to have me there, when she's hurting and she needs to know not everybody's a cold son of a bitch looking to use her. There's times she's like a little girl needing something to hold to, and I've always been what she's held to. I been with her since we was kids, since she was fifteen, and I ain't about to quit now."

"Keep it down, Red. You get hot under the collar, they'll hear you down there. And you got as much reason as me not to want them hearing you."

Red glanced over his shoulder at the cabin below, then back to Slocum. "You just stay off me and Dory, Cap'n, that's all. It ain't something you got a right to talk about."

A rattle of loose pebbles came from within the shaft, and Ramona pushed Dory out into the moonlight, still gagged, her hands still tied behind her back. The look of fear on her face changed when she saw Red; she glanced at Slocum, then back to Red's shotgun, and Slocum could almost see her pride returning in the way she cocked her head and presented her wrists to Ramona in the certain expectation of being untied.

When the rope was off and the gag removed, she turned to Red, rubbing the blood back into her wrists. "Where's the others? Does Ashe know you're up here?"

"No. They're palavering down there. Getting ready to read me out of this bunch, I think. I came out looking for you."

A sudden pleased grin split her face. "Good. Slocum said he hid the money under a cabin. You get it, Red, and let's ride out of here, just the two of us. Let the rest of them argue. We'll have the money."

"I already got it," Red said. "And riding out of here's just what I aim to do." He drew his Colt and handed it to her butt-first. "You get up on that horse and keep this thing trained on Slocum. I'll be with you in a minute."

While Dory mounted up, he broke open the shotgun and removed the shells. "Cap'n, I hate to leave you like this, but there's nothing I can do. I've seen you in tougher spots. Likely you can work your way out if they don't see you up here."

"He'll be all right even if they do see him up here," Dory said. "He's got the mine rigged like a fort. I saw it when I first got here—barrels of black powder all set to roll down that slope. With fuses and everything."

"Then that's a help," Red said "Let's hope you don't have to use them." He tossed the shotgun to the ground, unloaded Slocum's Colt, and started jacking the shells out of the Winchester. "Cap'n, I'll leave you these guns, the Colt and the shotgun and this rifle. Likely you'll need 'em."

"Red, don't be a fool," Dory said. "He'll try to follow us. You know that."

"He can't fire at us without bringing the others up here. And by the time he figures where we've gone, we'll be on a train and a hundred miles away. I won't leave an old friend helpless."

Ramona was watching from the shaft entrance, her face pale. Dory had reined the horse up against the cliff just beyond the shaft, her dress riding up her calves, her legs too short to reach the stirrups. As Red backed toward the horse, Slocum eyed the Colt in her hand, not sure he could trust her, thinking some perverse impulse might bring her to cause him trouble even now. He edged toward the guns on the ground, looking to make sure the rest of Greene's bunch was still in that first cabin. He saw vague figures moving around inside, but nothing unusual. He was just bending for the shotgun when Dory fired the Colt into the air.

The sudden shot cracked the silence, echoing around the canyon. Slocum hit the ground, rolling up with the useless shotgun to see Dory fighting to control the spooked horse, the Colt still smoking in her hand. Ramona had ducked into the shaft; Red was half turned toward Dory, staring at her.

"What the hell'd you do that for?"

"Get up here quick. I want them coming. Let Slocum hold them off till we're gone. Now get up here before they see us."

"Sorry, Cap'n." Red threw the shells to the ground and leaped for the horse. Dory had already started it toward the pines; he grabbed the pommel, running, almost being dragged, then heaved himself upward and stabbed a boot in the stirrup and swung up behind Dory. They were already out of sight in the trees, noiseless in the deep bed of pine needles, when Slocum heard shouts and the slap of a door down the slope and looked to see men spilling out of that first cabin.

He froze where he was, on his knees, the shotgun still useless in his hands, hoping they wouldn't make him out in the moonlight. But they didn't have to see him; they'd heard where the shot had come from, and they were already fanning out up the slope, coming at a run.

21

He snatched up the other guns and dived for the spot where Red had thrown the shells. He stuck the Colt in his waistband and searched quickly along the ground, found a shotgun shell, then another. Ramona had dashed from the mine and was on hands and knees in front of him, doing the same. A quick look showed the men from the cabin still coming at a run, but he couldn't tell whether they'd seen him yet. He shoved the shotgun shells into his pocket, found a rifle cartridge, then a .45 for the Colt, then two more rifle cartridges, then another a foot or two away. He heard somebody shout down below, and a shot sounded, the bullet whining overhead to splatter against the cliff face.

He grabbed Ramona by the arm. "Forget it. Back inside," and he lunged for the shaft.

He threw the shotgun down just inside and started shoving the cartridges he'd found into the Winchester. Ramona had scrambled in behind him. "I found some," she said, and he took two more from her, shoved them in and levered a round into the chamber.

"Find those ammunition boxes and have some more ready. I'm going to be too busy to reload myself."

He kicked one of the powder kegs over on its side and shrank up against the shaft wall where he could see out. They had spread out and slowed to a trot, just visible in the moonlight. No way of telling if it was from caution, or whether because he hadn't returned fire they weren't sure where he was or if it was even him. They must have noticed by now that Red was missing, though maybe not Dory. But that shot would bring them all the way up here, no matter what they thought, and he couldn't afford that. He drew down on the man in the center of the line, held his breath, squeezed off a shot. The man yelped and went down, but he could tell by the yell that the wound wasn't serious. Brief bright flashes came from along the line, and he ducked involuntarily as bullets thudded into the rock at the side of the shaft. They were running again, and he saw the man he'd hit get to his feet and hop one-legged toward the trees on the left. He brought the Winchester up again and fired off five shots as fast as he could work the lever, shifting fast from man to man along the line. One man went down, then they all hit the dirt, but he knew they were just taking cover, that he had missed, firing downhill and overshooting. But he had slowed them down, anyway.

He wheeled to hand Ramona the Winchester to reload, then knelt beside the powder keg he'd kicked over, fumbling in his pocket for the box of matches. He found the puncture he'd made in the keg, then the fuse, ran his fingers out along it till he found the end of it. He raked a match along his boot heel, and the sudden flare of flame lit up the shaft like a lamp. A sudden volley of fire came from below; bullets splattered the ceiling above his head, dust and rock chips raining down. He ducked down to touch the match to the fuse, watched it catch, then kicked the keg out and down the slope.

Ramona had the Winchester reloaded. He flicked the match out, handed her the Colt and the .45 shell. "Only one round for that, but load it anyway. We need everything we got." And he swung back to the entrance with the rifle.

The keg had bounced over the trolley rails and was rolling down the slope, bounding briefly into the air as it hit a little rise of ground, and rolling on. The men were on their feet again, darting out of its path, but he could tell they didn't know what it was; likely they thought it was a boulder—they were scattering only far enough to give it room to pass. He stopped breathing, his hearing suddenly acute, waiting for the blast—now, now—but it didn't come; the keg rolled and bounced on past them, and the line converged again, a rifle spat fire at him, and they came running up the slope, shouting now. He swore and settled his sights on a man in a light-colored shirt, fired, and swore with satisfaction this time as the man dropped like a stone.

The blast was deafening when it came. He saw a sudden explosive flash of light; an abrupt wave of concussive air hammered from cliff to cliff, hurting his ears and driving him instinctively down. When he looked again, only a wall still stood where the second cabin had been; timbers were spinning lazily through the air, and even from here he could hear the clash and spatter of debris striking the cabins on either side. There was no fire; there had been that one brief flash as it blew, but nothing after; the timbers clattered down into the debris, and now he saw that one last wall slowly sag in the moonlight, swaying down to collapse with a crash, leaving only the fireplace still standing.

Greene's bunch was flat on the ground, but he knew they weren't hurt; they were too far from the cabin to have been hit. They were just startled, stunned; they likely hadn't checked to see what was in these kegs, wouldn't have expected to face explosives from what they thought was a man alone and armed only with a rifle. He ducked back down and knocked another keg over on its side.

He struck another match, crouched down behind the keg, as if that would do any good—one lucky hit on the keg and this whole shaft would go up, taking him and Ramona with it. The glow of the match reflecting off the walls brought them alert down there; he heard more shouts and another rattle of rifle fire, but he forced himself to hold the flame to the fuse till it caught, crushed the match underfoot, and waited, waited, waited, watching the sputtering spark eat its way up the fuse, ducked as a bullet sang past his head to strike rock far back in the chamber, waited a moment longer, then got a boot under the keg and shoved it out of the mine.

This time they knew what it was. He had the Winchester up and firing again as they scattered to either side, making for the shelter of the pines. He saw one go down clutching his knee, but before he could get off another shot, the man had dragged himself into the trees. The keg hit a rock and leaped into the air, wobbling heavily end over end, and landed right in the center of where the line had been.

The blast blew a fountain of dirt twenty feet high; again there was that quick bright flash that seemed to light the ground for a hundred yards around, and the wave of sound that hammered the air of the shaft and echoed resoundingly around the canyon walls. Fragments of copper flicked through the trees on both sides of the blast. Slocum heard a man cry out on the right, but he couldn't see to tell how bad he was hurt; they were all out of sight, concealed in the timber. The last of the dirt spattered down through the branches. He heard no more cries, but there was no way of knowing how many casualties there were; they'd made it into the trees too fast.

They weren't firing now. They no longer had that straight line of fire into the mine, and likely they were regrouping; likely they would work up to the cliff and approach from the sides, where he wouldn't be able to see them coming without a risky look around the mouth of the shaft. The closer they got, the less chance he had to hold them off. He couldn't let them get to the face of that cliff.

He knelt to find the keg he'd wrapped the long fuses around, digging the shotgun shells out of his pocket and tossing them to Ramona. "Shove these in that shotgun when you've got the rifle loaded."

"I've only got five rifle shells left."

"No help for it. That'll have to do."

Working fast, he unwound the fuses to the charges and tipped the two remaining kegs onto their sides. He could see one body lying out on the slope; if the rest were still alive, that left five men he had to deal with. Probably six. He had counted on Red taking out the guard on the trail, but Red was smart enough to wait till this hullabaloo brought the man back down here. If Red didn't think of that, Dory would; the guard would be in a hurry to join this fight, and that would leave them a clear trail out.

The flare of the match drew no fire this time; likely they were concentrating on working up through the trees. He touched it to the fuses connected to those charges out there, hoping they hadn't been accidentally kicked loose by Dory or Red on their way up from the cabins. Then he lit the fuse on each of the remaining kegs and worked them as close to the mouth of the shaft as he dared, waiting, watching the fuses sputter. Then, aiming them as best he could toward the trees on either side, toward where he judged those men to be, he shoved them out and rolled to grab up the Winchester.

The bottle-charge on the right blew just as he looked out again, not as big a blast as he'd hoped, but it brought a shriek that said somebody had been hurt and the crackle of the rifle cartridges he'd dropped into the powder. The kegs were halfway to the trees, rolling heavily, beginning to arc away as gravity pulled them down the slope; then the canteen-charge on the left blew, louder that the first, and more rifle cartridges popped like firecrackers, and somebody yelled there, too, and a man broke out of the trees as if to escape them, nearly colliding with one of the unrushing powder kegs.

Both kegs exploded almost simultaneously. The flash lit up the trees, and great geysers of dirt shot skyward on either side. The man running from the left disappeared as if he'd never been, and Slocum thought his eardrums would burst from the concussion reverberating in the confined air of the shaft. When the echo had ricocheted away across the canyon, he could still hear dirt and copper fragments raining down through the trees. Then even that ceased, and there was nothing but silence, broken only by the frightened squealing of the horses down in the corral.

He crouched at the mouth of the shaft, waiting, listening. Neither of the kegs had gotten into the trees before it exploded. The blast might have carried far enough into the trees to be effective, but with the charges going off, likely those men had already been flat on the ground.

Two men dead that he knew about. That left four, counting the guard; he'd have had time to get here by now. At least two of them had been wounded earlier. And those bullets in the charges might have taken a toll. No way of telling if all four were still alive, but the odds were definitely better. And he didn't like the feeling of being trapped in this shaft, waiting for somebody to sneak up on him from the side. The time had come to take the fight to them. And for close-quarter fighting in those trees, he would need the shotgun.

He turned and started back into the mine, edging along the wall where the kegs had been. He couldn't see Ramona; she was somewhere farther back in the shaft. His foot encountered the lantern, and he bent to take it out of the way. He was just straightening up when he heard Ramona scream.

He dropped to the ground and rolled. He was trying to get turned, trying to bring the Winchester around, when he heard the *wham* of the shotgun behind him. The blast nearly deafened him; he felt the whoosh of the buckshot pass above his head, saw the shape of a man suddenly wrench away from the moonlit oval of the entrance, blown completely out of sight by the impact of the blast, gone as abruptly as he'd appeared, only the clatter of a rifle hitting the ground to say he had been there at all.

Slocum hugged the ground. He knew the man was dead, but that was a double-barreled shotgun; she could have fired only one barrel, might still have a nervous finger on the second trigger.

The air stank of gunpowder. Fine dust drifted down from the ceiling. The shaft seemed suddenly dead quiet now that the echoes had died away.

He heard the fear in her voice when she spoke: "Slocum? Slocum, did I hit you?"

"I'm all right. Over here."

He heard her creep up through the dark, dragging the shotgun; felt her touch his shoulder.

"I didn't even think," she said. "He jumped in front of the shaft, and I just pulled the triggers. I didn't even aim."

"Don't have to aim a shotgun at that distance. You did a good job. Another second, and he'd have had me."

He got to his knees, watching the entrance, listening hard, the Winchester ready now. The horses were still squealing down in the corral, but he couldn't hear anything else. That didn't mean much. This man had gotten to the shaft without making any noise. He brushed the dust from his face and rose to his feet. He was going to have to go out looking for them, and without a shotgun now. He still had five rounds in the Winchester. Not a lot, but he could maybe retrieve a gun from the man Ramona had killed. He'd heard a rifle hit the ground; it was likely ruined by the buckshot, but there might be a handgun that was all right.

"You think there's more left?" she said.

"Don't know. I'll have to go look."

"Is that safe?"

"No choice. We're trapped. We can't count on getting the next one that jumps in here. And you'll have to come with me. You can't stay here by yourself. You still got that Colt?"

"It's back there where I was."

"You bring that. I want to get a gun off the man you just shot. Stay here while I see if it's safe. I'll wave you out when I'm ready."

22

He moved stealthily back to the mouth of the shaft, hunkered down against the left wall, and risked a look outside. There was no light in any of the cabins now. He didn't remember the first cabin being dark when those men had spilled out of it; somebody, likely the Mex woman, had snuffed the lamps after the fight had started. The man Ramona had killed lay head down on the slope about ten feet in front of the mine, on his back, arms and legs spread wide. The horses in the corral were quiet now. He eased his head out of the shaft to check the cliff face on the left. Nobody there. Nobody on the other side, either. He drew his head back in and waited a moment. He had drawn no fire, and he'd heard nothing down in the trees. That didn't prove he hadn't been seen. But there was one way to find out. He took a deep breath and dived out of the shaft.

He hit the dirt and rolled to the right, coming up on his elbows, the Winchester already searching the trees. His ears seemed to strain, listening for a footfall, the click of a rifle being cocked, the rustle of a tree branch. An owl hooted somewhere up on top of the cliff. A dull whir on the left brought his head around, but it was only a bat, wheeling across the night sky. Otherwise, there was nothing.

He had landed about two yards to the right of the dead man. He'd felt his leg strike the man's rifle as he rolled; it was somewhere near his feet. Keeping his eyes on the trees, he felt around till he found it with his boot, dragged it up to where he could get a hand on it. The handgrip was shattered, and he was sure the mechanism was ruined; he could feel an unnatural kink in the metal just above the trigger housing. He pushed it aside and started elbowing his way over toward the body.

The buckshot had caught the man right in the midsection. His belly was a mass of blood and guts, and blood was already soaking the ground around him. His Colt was still in the holster; Slocum drew it out, checked to see that it was loaded, and thrust it down in his waistband. The gun belt was splattered with blood and bits of flesh. He removed a handful of shells from the cartridge loops on the sides and shoved them down in his pocket. Still no reaction from the trees. If any of those men were alive, they should be able to see him out here in the moonlight. But maybe they were waiting for him to get impatient and come to them. They could afford to wait for a sure shot on their own ground. He turned and crawled back toward the mine.

Ramona was waiting just inside the shaft. He edged in beside her and handed her the cartridges he'd taken off the body.

"Those are for the Colt. When you're ready, we're going to work our way along the cliff to the left. I think most of them headed for the trees over there."

"Do you think they're still alive?"

"They're not moving if they are. But some of them could be playing possum."

He scanned the terrain while she loaded the Colt. The man he'd killed first, when they were still charging up toward the mine, lay halfway down the slope. Just short of the trees on the left lay the man killed by the powder keg. Three dead. Three possibly still alive. At least one of those was in the trees on the right, but he was wounded, and likely pretty bad judging by that shriek when the charge had gone off. Two of the men on the left had had leg wounds. It was possible they were hurt too bad to move, but that didn't mean they couldn't fire a gun. And one of those might have been the man killed by the blast of the powder keg; there might still be a man unhurt on the left, able to move around and pick his spot.

He heard the cylinder click closed on the Colt and turned to see Ramona's eyes on him, her face pale.

"I'm ready," she said.

"We're going to have to cover the trees on both sides," he said. "I'm going out slow, and I want you to keep your back to mine. You'll have to walk backwards, but you'll have the cliff face to guide yourself by. I'll watch the trees in front of me. You watch behind us. You see anything fishy, shoot it. Can you do that?"

She nodded, looking down, the Colt clutched in both hands.

"All right, then. Let's go."

He took one look all around the slope, but he saw nothing that hadn't been there before. Then he slipped out around the corner and started along the base of the cliff.

He kept it very slow, one foot in front of the other, watching the trees. He sensed Ramona behind him, backing carefully; her heel struck his boot and she gave a little lurch, righted herself, and continued on. There was still no sign of life in the pines, but he was sure he could be seen against the cliff face, bare-chested as he was, and Ramona's white legs had to show up in the moonlight. Then a sound from the front brought him to a halt. Ramona bumped up against him, and he felt her hand come around to touch his back, but she didn't turn. He strained to see in the dark, but there was nothing out there but empty ground. Now he heard it off to the right, an airy whisper of wings: the bat again. He released the breath he'd been holding in and started on.

It seemed to take forever till they reached the first of the pines, but they made it without mishap. He led her on another twenty yards into the dark under the trees

along the cliff, then halted and pulled her down beside
him. The moonlight was fainter here; at least they'd be
harder to see.

"It'll be trickier now. There may be a man laying up
in there waiting for us. We might not see him till we're
right on him. Are you all right?"

She nodded, quiet and subdued, eyes on the timber
down the slope.

"Stay close to me," he said. "And try not to make
any noise."

It was even darker down in the timber; he could
barely make out the flash of Ramona's legs off to his
left. The acrid smell of blasting powder still hung in the
air. Here and there a tree trunk showed a pale gash of
raw wood where a copper fragment had cut through the
bark. The pine needles kept things quiet underfoot; then
the pine needles gave way to fresh dirt, and he knew
they were approaching the site where he'd buried that
canteen full of black powder. A few steps farther on he
saw the hole up ahead, a crater in the ground where the
charge had gone off. He crouched down behind a tree
trunk and let his eyes adjust to the terrain, picking out
what detail he could.

The crater was about four feet across. Dirt was
mounded up around the edges, but he could see a body
on the ground just beyond it. The man was lying on his
belly, facing the crater, and he wasn't moving. He
looked dead enough, but he mig... just be hurt and
unable to move, playing dead to draw Slocum closer.

Ramona had come up beside him. "Stay here and
cover for me," he whispered. "I'll check to see if he's
alive."

He left the Winchester with her, drew the Colt from
his waistband, and faded a yard or two off to the right.
Then he dropped to his belly and began to crawl around
the edge of the crater. When he got close, he could tell
the man wasn't playing possum; the arms were flung
out wide, and there was no gun in either hand. He

halted for a moment, searching the dark; when he was fairly sure there was nobody else lurking in the trees, he crawled across to the body and turned it over on its back.

He didn't have to check the pulse to know the man was dead. The face was barely human, nothing but a mass of blood and meat; he must have been right over the charge when it went off. There was no sign of a gun; likely it was buried under the dirt somewhere. Slocum scanned the trees again. Then he turned and waved Ramona up.

He returned the Colt to his waistband and took the Winchester from her. "One left over here if I'm counting right. Good odds, but he may be desperate. Stick closer to me."

The dirt from the blast extended another few feet down the slope, and then they were on pine needles again, moving from tree to tree, pausing behind a tree trunk to search the timber ahead, then moving on to the next. If there was a man left alive in here, he had to know he was alone; the swift decimation of the others should have left him shaken, and maybe careless. And maybe trigger-happy.

They were a little more than halfway down through the timber when he heard a sudden rush of noise ahead of him. He grabbed Ramona and threw her to the ground, landing half on top of her; then he rolled away and came up with the Winchester cocked, trying to locate the sound. Footsteps, moving at a run, away from him, down through the trees. He leaped to follow, dodging a tree trunk, skidding in the pine needles, still unable to see anything in the dark.

The man had broken out into the open and was running for the cabins by the time Slocum reached the edge of the trees. He threw himself up against a slender pine and got off a fast shot, missed, and tried for another; the rifle jammed, and he swore, jacked the lever till he'd cleared the jam, and looked for his target again. Too late—the man had already rounded a corner down there, and that was the cabin where Quinn had left his horse; he would never get to him now. He shifted the Winchester to the right, aiming across the debris of the cabin leveled by the first powder blast, heard the horse start up, saw it clear that still-standing chimney, tracked it till it was almost to the next cabin in line, and fired and missed again. Then it was out of sight, gone into the dark, hooves drumming across the hard ground toward the trail up the south face.

Slocum lowered the Winchester. Whoever it was had lost his nerve at the last minute, but he couldn't blame him for that, not after all the killing that had gone on down here.

He heard a noise behind him and wheeled, but it was Ramona coming down out of the dark.

"Is he gone?" she said.

"Started up the trail by now. I don't think he liked the odds."

"Are there any left?"

"One more, by my count. He was in the trees to the right of the mine, and hurt, too, I think. I'll have to go look for him. You want to stay here?"

She was still clutching the Colt, but she hugged herself, as if suddenly cold, looking back up toward where they'd found the last body. "I'd rather go with you. I don't want to be alone out here."

"There's a chance he's still alive. And we'll have to cross that open ground to the trees on the other side."

"I've come this far. A little more won't matter."

"All right. Let's get this thing over with."

They found the last man dead where the other charge had gone off. Slocum had figured he was either dead or hurt too bad to move when they made the dash across that open ground without drawing any fire. He wasn't hard to find; he was lying just inside the trees and down the slope a ways from where the second charge had been. He had taken a bullet from the charge right through the lungs, and he was lying on his back, legs twisted under him, glazed eyes staring at the sky. A large copper fragment had sliced into him about where his liver would be, but likely he'd already been hit by then, already dead. He was hatless and bearded; Slocum couldn't be sure in the moonlight, but he thought it was the man called Fox.

Ramona had waited down in the timber while he had come up to check the body; now he worked his way back to find her leaning against a tree, the Colt dangling in one hand.

"He's dead," he said. "That's the last of them."

He took the Colt from her, thrust it into his waistband with the other one, and was surprised to find her suddenly up against him, trembling, her arms around his waist.

"It's all right," he said, feeling awkward, back in a situation with her he'd put out of his mind, suddenly brought aware of her body again—her breasts pillowed against his chest, her slim back under his hands. "It's all right. It's all over."

She had her arms locked fiercely around him, her head laid against his shoulder, and he could feel the trembling running through her, as if she'd been holding fear in all night, maybe all day, and couldn't contain it now that there was nothing left to fear. She clung to him like that for a while, then relaxed her hold and leaned back to look up at him.

"Thank you," she said, and he could feel the trembling subside a little.

"We haven't got much time," he said. "I want to see if I can catch Dory and Red before they get clean away, but I have to get you back to Bowie first. That means we'll have to ride all night. Are you game for that?"

"If we have to. After this, I can do anything."

"Good. I had what's left of your dress when Red caught me. It's in the trees on the other side. We'll pick it up and then go saddle those horses in the corral. I'm going to take these bodies into Bowie to show your Mr. Boldt. I'm not sure he'd take my word for what happened out here.''

They retrieved the dress and started toward the corral. Near the corner of the cabin they'd been tied up in he found a saddled horse, reins dangling, the mount of the man who'd been standing guard at the top of the trail; he'd made it down here just in time to get himself killed. Slocum led it on up to the corral and found Dooley's body there, under a blanket beside the gate, where the others had laid it out when they'd come back in at sunset. Six bodies, then; that ought to satisfy even a man like Boldt. While Ramona set to work on the dress, trying to get it fit enough to wear, he carried a bridle in through the gate and began stalking the horses.

His own gray was there; he saddled it first. Greene's horse was still down in front of the first cabin. He figured they could pick it up on the way out; Ramona could ride it. He would have to stop down there for his war bag and bedroll, anyway. When he had enough horses saddled, he cut lengths of rope from a coil hanging off one of the saddle horns and fashioned a lead for each, one behind the other. He left the gate open on the one horse left in the corral, so it could find its way out when it felt the need for water.

Ramona had torn off the bodice of the dress and put the skirt of it on, the shirt knotted at her waist for a top. ''What do you think happened to the woman?''

''The cabin that went up was the one she shared with Greene. If she was in there, she's dead for sure. If she's alive, she's probably hiding somewhere. She'll get to this horse after we're gone. She'll be all right.''

It took them the better part of an hour to load up, leading the string of horses from body to body. Slocum identified the ones he could as he hoisted them aboard—Fox and Runnion and Ashe Greene. It was Greene that Ramona had killed with the shotgun, in front of the mine shaft. The only one he couldn't locate was Sandy Quinn. The man killed by the canteen-charge had blondish hair, but with the face virtually blown off, there was no way to identify him for sure; it might have been Quinn who had bolted for the horse and made it out unhurt.

The bodies lashed on, the Winchester stashed in the gray's saddle scabbard, they led the string back down the slope and around to where Greene's horse stood tethered to the rail in front of the first cabin. The pile of timbers and debris beside the cabin looked eerie in the moonlight, the fireplace chimney rising up out of it like a grave marker. Slocum wondered if the Mex woman was somewhere under that debris. He untied Greene's horse, shortened the stirrups, and boosted Ramona up into the saddle.

"Some of my stuff's inside," he said. "Wait here while I get it."

He had just ducked under the hitching rail and started onto the porch when he heard a warning cry from Ramona and the creak of the door swinging suddenly open.

He froze, one boot on the first step, a hand on the porch support. The woman stood in the doorway, sighting across a Colt held in both hands and pointing right at him.

Everything stopped inside him. He couldn't see her expression; it was too dark under the porch for that. He was very careful not to move, but his mind was working again, coming suddenly unstuck after the shock.

He kept his voice very soft: "It won't do you any good. Your man's already dead. They're all dead. All but one, and he rode out and left you."

She didn't move. The Colt didn't even waver.

"All I want is my things," he said. "My bedroll and my war bag. You know they're in there."

Still she didn't move. But she didn't fire, either. He figured she was scared; if she was set on killing him, she would have done it by now.

"I left you a horse in the corral. We're going to leave the canyon soon as I get my things. Once we're gone, you can get that horse and ride out. There must be someplace you can go."

For a long moment she stayed where she was, looking at him, the Colt out at arm's length. Then, slowly, she lowered her hands and took a step back into the cabin. He waited for the length of a breath, chanced a step forward, then another. She moved back into the cabin with every step he took, watching him, the Colt still clutched in both hands but pointing at the floor now. When he reached the door he glanced to the left to make sure his war bag was still there. Keeping his eyes on her, he sidestepped along the wall, groped with a hand till he found the bedroll beside the war bag. She watched him as he bent to pick them up and edged back toward the door. She was still standing there when he backed across the porch and down the steps to the horses.

Still facing the cabin, he handed the bedroll up to Ramona. "Hang onto this till we get away from here." He had the eerie sensation that the woman wouldn't make a move as long as she could see he was watching her; he backed along Ramona's horse till he found the gray, eased around it, and swung up into the saddle, the war bag hanging heavily from one hand. "Take it slow. Just put the horse to a walk. And once you're past the porch, don't look back."

He waited till he was sure Ramona had cleared the corner of the cabin, then he nudged the gray in the ribs and started after her, the string of body-laden horses following along behind.

He didn't relax till they had gone two hundred yards through the dark and he knew they were out of sight. He had stayed behind Ramona all the way, keeping the gray between her and the cabin, the skin of his back prickling in expectation of a bullet long after they were out of pistol range. He didn't really believe the woman would fire at them even if she had a rifle in there, but the skin of his back didn't seem convinced. When he was sure it was safe, he signaled Ramona to halt and swung down out of the saddle.

"Will she follow us, do you think?" Ramona said.

"No reason to. She's got her own problems." He took the bedroll from her and tied it on behind his own saddle. "Our only worry now is whether the man that ran is laying up for us at the top of the cliff. If he thinks we have the money, he might decide it's worth another try."

He searched through the war bag till he found himself a shirt; he'd already taken a hat from one of the bodies. The Mex woman had packed his gun belt in the war bag too; he strapped it on, glad to have a holster for his Colt again. He tucked the second Colt down through the belt and swung back into the saddle.

"I'll go first, in case he's waiting for us. You'll have to lead the other horses. The trail is awful narrow in spots—if they start acting up on you, let go of the lead rope. Better to lose them than to get pulled off that cliff."

When they reached the base of the cliff, he drove the gray up the first twenty yards of the trail, then halted and looked back. The moonlight, reflecting off rock, was brighter here. Ramona had started up behind him, sitting very erect, hanging on to the saddle horn. He could tell she was scared, but she had already proved she could do a difficult thing even through her fear. The only problem might come if one of the horses got spooked or strayed too close to the edge and started slipping off. If one went, the whole string would go, tied together the way they were. And even if she released the lead rope, her own horse might get spooked by the others, and there wasn't much room to control a spooked horse up here.

The trail was barely wide enough; the bodies draped over the saddles were just brushing against the cliff face, but there was room. When he was sure she was all right, he turned in the saddle and nudged the gray on.

They were about two-thirds of the way up when he reined in the gray and eased down out of the saddle. There was just room enough to stand beside the horse, but the drop-off was not so steep here; the trail was bordered on the left by the tips of pines growing up and out from the rock below. He worked his way back to take Ramona's horse by the bridle.

"I'm going to take a look around on top. You'd better dismount and come up in front of the horse. If there's shooting, the horses may get to rearing, and you'll want to be out of the way."

He waited till she'd slipped to the ground and come up to take the reins. Then he slid the Winchester out of the scabbard and started on up, leading the gray this time.

He left the horse when he neared the top and went on alone, quiet and careful. He was close enough to see where the trail broke out onto flat ground. Not enough cover to shield anybody there. Maybe that boulder up on the right, but anybody coming up the trail would be almost on you there before you saw them. No, if the man was here, he would be back in the trees where he could get a clear shot as soon as a horse or a man came out onto the bluff. Otherwise, he would have picked them off halfway down the cliff. Slocum eased up out of the trail and put the boulder between him and the trees, letting his eyes adjust to the terrain.

The pines reared up dark and tall against the night sky. Moonlight barely filtered through. He scanned the shadows along the bluff, glancing from tree trunk to tree trunk, trying to find a shape that shouldn't be there. If the man was here, he was well hid. He took his eyes off the trees and concentrated on sounds, listening for the restless stir of a horse, a click of metal, a body shifting position. Nothing but a faint breeze in the treetops. He waited five minutes, watching, listening, before he decided there was only one way to be sure. When he was set, he dodged out from behind the boulder and sprinted for the nearest tree.

He landed up against its trunk and held his breath, listening. Still nothing; and he'd drawn no fire. He eased around the trunk and dashed for a tree farther into the timber.

Moving from tree to tree, he covered a stretch maybe twenty yards deep and forty wide before he was sure there was no one there. Whoever the man was, he'd evidently decided the game wasn't worth the risk. There was a chance he was laying in wait farther down the slope, but Slocum didn't think so. This was the place to stage an ambush if that was what you had in mind. With Greene and the rest dead, all this man had in mind was putting a lot of ground between him and the canyon. Slocum left the trees and went back to get the gray.

Ramona led the other horses out behind him. He took the lead rope from her and fastened it to the leather ties hanging off the rear of his saddle.

"Clear trail from here on," he said, "but it's going to be a hard ride. I want to reach Bowie by morning and then set out after Red and Dory."

"Right away?"

"Have to, to catch them. I've gone that long without sleep before. Red said something about him and Dory catching a train. You know where the nearest railhead is?"

"Daley City, south of here. There's another town in between, Painted Rock, but there's not even a stage station there."

"How far is Daley City?"

"A little more than a day's ride, I think."

"Well, they'll likely overnight somewhere in between. There's a chance, anyway. Let's get started."

In the saddle again, they set out down through the trees, heading for the trail that would lead them to the dry riverbed and the road to Bowie. Slocum settled himself in the saddle and let the gray pick its own pace. It was going to be a long night.

23

Bowie came in sight about two hours after dawn, its bleak buildings already baking in the morning sun, the one wide street a dusty white under a blazing blue sky.

Slocum had kept the gray close up beside Ramona's horse all through the night, ready to catch her when sleep started bringing her out of the saddle. She rode slumped over the saddle horn, the dress riding up her bare legs, her unshod feet barely reaching the stirrups. He would watch her nod into a drowse and ride a ways fully asleep, rocking to the gentle gait of the horse; then she would begin to slip sideways, still sleeping, and he would catch her then, and she would right herself with a start and ride on awake for a while, only to begin that long slow descent into sleep again. He had no idea how many times he had drifted off himself, only the memory of jerking awake to find himself still plodding across that barren wasteland in the moonlight.

Dawn had brought them both awake, the huge sun rising hot and bright over the tableland to the east and making sleep impossible. Now, with the town up ahead, the horses quickened the pace, sensing water and grain not too far off.

The town looked as deserted as it had the first day he'd seen it. A buggy was just heading east out of town, and one man leaned against a porch railing on the north side of the street, but the street itself was empty. Slocum checked the horses straggling along behind him, each one carrying a body draped across it. He figured they made quite a picture coming in sight over that hot white plain: Ramona with her bare legs showing and a man's shirt knotted around her waist, one sleeve torn away; and six corpses strung out in a line, arms and legs dangling down opposite sides of their mounts.

The man on the porch evidently thought so, too. When they were close enough to make out, he descended into the street, shading his eyes to get a better look. He stood spraddle-legged in the dust for a long moment, as if uncertain he was actually seeing what he thought he saw; then he broke into a run, heading for the marshal's office. He wasn't in there a minute before he came back out and trotted down the boardwalk toward Boldt's place.

The marshal was waiting for them when they drew up before the jail. He was standing by the hitching rail, hands on his hips, head cocked up under his hat as if he, too, wasn't sure what he'd been looking at was real.

Slocum doffed his hat. "Morning, Marshal."

Brady nodded to Ramona and touched a hand to his own hat. "I never expected to see you again."

"Why?" Slocum said. "You think I'm not a man that keeps his word?"

"Don't know you well enough to say that. But, generally, you tell me a man's riding out of here with forty thousand dollars in his saddlebags, which forty thousand belongs to somebody else, and I don't expect to see him again. Especially when he sends the men put on his trail back to town with their tails between their legs."

"That was just a little reminder to Boldt that we agreed I'd work alone. When I set out to do something, I generally do it."

"Well, seems you did it—I can't deny that. That is Greene's bunch, ain't it?"

"All but two of them. And now if you're satisfied, we'll be heading down to see Sam Boldt. We been riding all night, and we're tired."

"Miss Ramona, you want to get down?" Brady was eyeing her torn dress and the sleeveless shirt, as if speculating on what had happened to put her in that garb. "You could wait here if you'd like."

"I thank you, Marshal, but no. A few more yards won't hurt."

Slocum nudged the gray in the ribs, and they started on, the marshal keeping pace along the boardwalk. Boldt had come out on the porch of the Drover's Hotel, along with the man who'd gone to fetch him. When they got close, Slocum saw it was Nolan, the man Boldt had put on his trail with Matt Walker. He reined in at the rail in front of the hotel, and Boldt and Nolan came down the steps into the dust of the street.

Boldt glanced at Slocum, then went to help Ramona down from her horse. "Slocum, you have my apology for sending men after you. But you can understand my position. Was it who I thought it was?"

"Ashe Greene's bunch," Slocum said. "That's Greene on that first horse."

One arm around Ramona, Boldt eyed the string of bodies with something like satisfaction. "Marshal, lay them out in the street. Right in front of the jail. Let people see what happens to men that cross Sam Boldt. Ramona, I got the cook hauling hot water upstairs—you likely want a bath. And you look like you could use a drink, Slocum."

"If it's all the same to you, I'd like to stable my horse first. It needs to be fed and watered and rubbed down. I aim to ride out of here this morning."

He saw Brady and Nolan exchange a glance, but Boldt only nodded. If a man could be trusted to take $40,000 out alone and still come back, he could be trusted a bit longer. Slocum wondered how trusting Boldt would be when he learned the money was gone.

"I'll see you upstairs when you're finished," Boldt said. "Nolan, when you got the bodies off, run those other horses into a corral out back." And he led Ramona up the steps and into the hotel.

Nolan gave Slocum one last hard look, as if he didn't

like the way this was being handled, but he didn't say anything, just took the lead rope and turned the horses back toward the jail. Brady lingered a moment, like maybe he was thinking it best to keep an eye on Slocum himself, but then he, too, turned and started back along the boardwalk.

In the stable, Slocum unsaddled the gray and directed the hostler to feed and water it and rub it down. Then he lit a cheroot from his war bag and watched to see that it was done right, wondering what he was going to tell Sam Boldt. He had brought Boldt's woman back—that was the main thing—and with her backing him up, Boldt would have no reason not to believe him about what had happened. But there was a chance Boldt might send somebody out to track Red and Dory down, trying to get the ransom back, and he didn't want that. He could handle Red, but if Red got cornered by a couple of Boldt's men, he would shoot it out and likely get himself killed. And if there was anything to be salvaged from this whole thing, it was that promise to get Red home to his family before his daddy died.

The hostler had a feed bag on the gray and was rubbing it down with an old saddle blanket. Slocum took a last drag on the cheroot and ground it out underfoot. When he looked up, Nolan was standing in the doorway, hands propped on his gun belt.

"You forgot Mr. Boldt wants to see you?" Nolan said.

"I figured you'd remind me," Slocum said, and shouldered past him. "You been a messenger boy so long, Nolan, you've forgot there's men that ain't."

"Just doing my job," Nolan said.

Slocum ignored him, circling the stable onto Main Street and crossing the dust to the hotel. The lobby was empty except for a bartender washing down the mirror behind the bar. Nolan led him up the stairs to the second floor and rapped on the second door along the hall.

Boldt opened it and waved Slocum inside. "You wait in the office, Nolan."

This time Slocum found himself in a large sitting room, the morning sun coming in the windows along the opposite wall. The doors into the office were on the left; another door on the right, closed now, evidently led into more of Boldt's suite. He followed Boldt to a couple of stuffed chairs, where a tray bearing a bottle and two glasses sat on a small table.

Boldt splashed a glass half full of whiskey and handed it to him. "You look like you could use that."

"Thanks." Slocum took the drink and sank into one of the chairs. "Ramona tell you what happened?"

"Didn't ask her. She's in there taking a bath. I wanted to hear it from you."

Slocum skipped the run-in with Nolan and Walker; they would have informed Boldt about that. And he for sure wasn't going to tell about being tied half-naked on a bunk with Ramona and what had followed from it. He watched Boldt's face while he told the rest, but nothing in Boldt's expression betrayed what he thought about it, and he didn't say anything until Slocum reported how Red and Dory had got away with the ransom.

Then: "I thought this Red Wylie was a friend of yours."

"He is. But seventeen years is a long time, and Dory's got quite a hold on him."

Boldt studied his face, as if to judge how much truth there might be in all that. "You wait here," he said, and disappeared through the door on the right.

Through the windows in the opposite wall, Slocum could see the sun advancing up the sky. He would have to get out of here soon if he was going to catch Red and Dory. Boldt had told Nolan to wait in the office next door, and Matt Walker was sure to be around somewhere; if Boldt decided to hold him here while they set out after Red, likely he would find himself back in Marshal Brady's jail. He might have to bring things to a showdown to prevent that, and given his lack of sleep, he wasn't sure how effective he could be.

The door on the right opened, and Boldt came back in with Ramona. She was wearing a loose, flowing robe, her wet hair bound up in a towel wrapped around her head. Boldt sat her down across from Slocum and took his own chair again.

"Slocum here just told me what happened. Now I want you to tell me. And no interruptions, Slocum. Let her tell it her own way."

Ramona glanced at Slocum, as if to judge what the situation was, then back to Boldt. Her story differed only in minor details from Slocum's, but when she had finished, Boldt said, "You sure this man hasn't tricked you in some way? You know he and Wylie and Dory were all old friends."

"He didn't trick me, Sam. I was there the whole time."

Boldt was silent then, thinking, gazing off toward the windows.

"I figure Red's not going to get any of that money," Slocum said. "Dory's too smart for him. She's got him hoodwinked. She'll ditch him before long and take it all for herself. You aim to send somebody after them?"

Boldt was silent for a moment longer. "No. No, I guess not. Dory was pretty upset when she left here. Claimed I was treating her bad. I suppose there's some truth in that. Maybe she's right. Maybe I owe her."

"Well, I'm going after them. I got some unfinished business with Red, anyway. They said something about catching a train. You have any idea when there'll be a train through Daley City?"

"There'll be a train or two through there tomorrow night," Boldt said. "Won't be another for a week after that. I suppose you might catch them."

"Well, if you got no more questions, I'll be going, then."

Boldt and Ramona accompanied him to the door. He

shook hands with Boldt, and then Ramona pressed his hand in both of hers, her stance putting Boldt just behind her, where he couldn't see. "Thanks for everything," she said, and the pressure on his hand and the smile she gave him told him what the "everything" included.

He retrieved his gray from the stable, lashed the war bag and bedroll on behind the saddle, and mounted up again, glad to be putting the town of Bowie behind him. Nolan was on the porch of the Drover's Hotel as he passed, and when he approached the west end of town, the marshal came out to watch him leave. The six bodies he had brought in were laid out in a row in front of the jail, baking in the hot morning sun. Boldt wasn't going to enjoy that sight long; a few more hours in that sun and he would have to put them underground.

Slocum nodded to the marshal, touched a hand to his hat, and put the gray into a trot.

24

He left the road just outside of town, cutting southwest across the prairie. He figured Red and Dory had aimed straight south from the canyons, along the road to Daley City, the nearest railhead. They had likely bedded down after two or three hours, once they were sure they weren't being pursued, but they would be on the road again by now. Riding double, they wouldn't be able to maintain much of a pace; if they had set out at dawn this morning they should reach Painted Rock, the only town between the canyons and Daley City, at about sunset. They would likely shop around there for a second horse, and that would delay them some. If he was lucky they would overnight in Painted Rock and head on tomorrow morning for Daley City, about three hours' ride farther on.

Riding across country, he could reach Painted Rock at about ten tomorrow morning, just about the time they would hit Daley City. But from what Boldt had said, there were no trains out of there till evening; he ought to catch up to them before they could get away.

The country was fairly flat here, dry and dusty, dotted with cactus and sagebrush. He kept the gray at a steady trot, wanting to cover as much ground as possible before nightfall. He had already gone twenty-four hours without sleep, but he could go another ten or twelve without it if he had to. He couldn't afford to lose time, and he had learned long ago, back in the war, that a man could function on very little sleep if the stakes were high enough.

The war. You would think that after nearly twenty years a man could leave behind him even something as big as a war. But lately he had begun to realize that what he was now had been formed by that war, and by the aftermath of it, and that what he was now was never going to change. He remembered when Red had suggested they hit that Yankee train, back in Georgia in '65, after Appomattox, and how he had felt then that his life was taking a momentous turn, heading in a direction he hadn't expected, and how there had seemed little he could do about it. He hadn't known then that it was going to lead him to years of aimless drifting, moving ever farther west as the frontier crept up behind him, till now he was no longer young and no longer believed he could change the life he led, no longer expected to find over the next hill anything different from what he'd seen over the last one. He sensed that that was what drove him now: He maybe couldn't change his own life, but he might be able to save what was left of Red's if he could get him home to his family before it was too late. Red's daddy had argued long and hard against their hitting that train back in Georgia, warning where that kind of thing could lead. He had certainly been right about Red, and Slocum figured he could make it up some if Red got to Oregon before the old man died.

Night was coming on when the need for sleep finally caught up with him. He made camp down near a little river, under a line of cottonwoods. The sky was clear and beginning to sparkle with stars as he wrapped himself in his bedroll, thinking that if he was right Dory and Red would be settling down in a hotel room in Painted Rock just about now, and unable to keep out of his mind the pictures of what was likely going on there, what had likely gone on when they'd bedded down last night in some campsite similar to this one, pictures of Dory naked and eager, using that voluptuous body and all the fierce skill she had to bind Red tighter to her, to blind him to the fact that she would betray him a little farther down the road, as she had so many times before. Dory would hang onto Red just so long as she figured he was useful to her, and no longer. And as Slocum fell asleep, he thought again of Georgia in '65, Dory at fifteen or sixteen creeping down the lean-to roof under her window, naked under her flannel nightgown, and how he had decided to break it off with her and how truculent Red had been about taking up with her himself, no matter what it meant. Seventeen years ago. Strange how long the consequences could be of what seemed at the time a simple act.

He was up at dawn, the gray saddled and on the trail again before half an hour had passed. He ate some cold beef jerky as he rode, not wanting to take the time to cook something up, and in an hour he struck the road running down from the canyon country and turned south onto it, toward Painted Rock. He figured he was about an hour ahead of schedule; if Red and Dory had spent the night in Painted Rock, they couldn't be far ahead; he would reach Daley City not too long after they did.

The sun wasn't very high in the sky when he saw a man afoot up ahead, walking along the right side of the road. He still had the gray at a trot, and when the man heard the sound of the horse, he stopped and turned, and Slocum saw it was Red, waiting for the gray to come up, his hands in his pockets.

Slocum reined in beside him. Red looked a little sheepish. His holster was empty; his clothes were dusty and wrinkled and looked like they'd been slept in, and he had trouble meeting Slocum's eye.

"Well," he said, "I can't say you didn't warn me."

"She set you afoot, did she?"

"Yesterday morning. Woke up and found her gone. Took the money and the horse and everything there was. Even took my gun. I been walking ever since."

Slocum felt a little weary, and not just from having only one night's sleep out of the last two. In the harsh bright light of a desert morning, Red looked even older than he was, his face gaunt and strained, his neck rising thin out of his dirty collar. He was making an attempt to be cheerful, but the most he could manage was a sheepish half grin that had more shame than humor in it, his tongue working in nervous twitches along his teeth, his eyes trying to hold on Slocum's but unable to keep from darting away.

"She headed for Daley City?" Slocum said.

"That's what we was planning on. She said we'd take a train south, till we could make a connection going west. We was aiming to go to California. Set up a place of business there."

"She left you yesterday morning. How far back along the road?"

"About a day's ride back. Maybe less. I figure she got to Painted Rock some time yesterday afternoon." His eyes made that effort to meet Slocum's again. "You ain't got something to chew on, have you? I ain't eat since day before yesterday."

"Got some beef jerky." Slocum kicked a boot loose from the stirrup. "You get up here behind me, and we'll see if we can get to Daley City in time. See if we can get some of that money back."

Red looked down and scuffed the dirt with his boot. "No hard feelings?"

"We go back a long way, Red. I maybe should have talked you loose from Dory Baker way back in '65, in Georgia. So maybe I owe you. Besides, I told your daddy I'd send you home to Oregon. You agree to that, why, we'll forget all the rest."

"Well," Red said, "going home to Oregon may be a good idea." He stuck a boot in the stirrup, reached to take Slocum's hand, and hauled himself up behind the saddle.

They rode into Painted Rock about two hours before noon. It wasn't much of a town, no bigger than Bowie, and Slocum figured the best place to ask for information would be the livery stable. If Dory had spent the night here, she would have stabled the horse, and the livery man would know when she retrieved it and set out for Daley City.

The liveryman was a short, plump man with a fringe of gray hair around a gleaming bald head. He said a woman like the one Slocum described had stabled her horse there the day before, maybe two, maybe three in the afternoon. Planned to ride on, she'd said, as soon as the man showed up that was supposed to meet her here.

"Supposed to meet her here?" Red said.

"That's what she said." The liveryman took a look in his entry book. "Stabled the horse overnight. Had a man with her when she paid this morning. Young fella. Blondish, blue-eyed. They rode out together about three hours ago."

Red looked at Slocum and started to say something, but Slocum took him by the arm and steered him out of the stable. Outside on the dusty back street, Red shook his arm free. "That's got to be Sandy Quinn," he said. "You didn't get him with them black-powder kegs, that's for sure."

"Evidently not. Only how did he know to meet her here?"

Red was staring off along the street, hands jammed in his pockets, a woeful look on his face. "She must have set it up with him before things went wrong. He'd cover for her, and if they got split up, why, they'd meet here in Painted Rock. That's the only thing I can figure."

"Well, she's got a gun hand with her now. If I know the effect Dory has on men, he'll risk his neck to protect her. So we're going to have to ride into Daley City with our eyes open."

"Hurts," Red said. "Knowing she never did have any idea to go off with me. Lying to me all the time."

"You ain't cured of her yet, are you?"

"No. No, I guess not. A man's a fool, ain't he? When it comes to women?"

"I figure that's something our young friend, Sandy Quinn, is going to learn soon enough. Come on, let's get to Daley City before that money leaves the country."

Daley City lay out on a treeless plain, three dusty streets, each a couple of blocks long, lined with high false-fronted buildings baking in the hot afternoon sun. It was bigger than Bowie and Painted Rock put together, with several cheap saloons scattered out along the road at either end of it, and a collection of cattle pens on the south edge of town. There was a lively traffic along the central street, wagons and buggies and knots of pedestrians, the ladies holding their skirts up out of the dust. Slocum brought the gray in along a back street and checked in at the stable, but the liveryman there hadn't seen anybody that sounded like Dory or Sandy Quinn.

"What do we do now?" Red said.

"Let's check the train depot. There's no trains out till evening, but they maybe already bought themselves tickets. And keep your eyes open. We want to see them before they see us."

The train depot was on the southwest end of town, complete with a little platform under the roof's overhang. Slocum had given Red one of the Colts he'd gotten off of Greene's bunch, and they had split up on the way from the stable, each of them taking a different side of the street. Slocum had paced along the boardwalk, keeping an eye on the crowd and on Red working his way along the opposite boardwalk, but he had seen no sign of Dory or Quinn by the time the depot came in sight. It sat off by itself, an adobe building with a peaked roof, about thirty yards beyond where the boardwalks gave out. Slocum crossed the street to join up with Red, and they edged up against the corner of the last building on the boardwalk, where they could get a look at the area around the depot.

"I didn't see 'em anywhere," Red said.

"Neither did I, but they're here somewhere. Watch the street."

He leaned idly against the building, his hat low, examining the depot platform out of the corner of his eye. From where he stood, the tracks lay along the left of the platform. About fifty yards to the left of the tracks, across a stretch of bare ground, were the cattle pens, empty now. Two freight wagons were butted up against the far end of the platform, but there were no prospective passengers in sight, only a Mexican slumped asleep against one wall, sombrero down over his eyes, and an old Indian woman squatted around the corner from him, selling beaded leather goods, her wares set out in baskets in front of her. He could see into the little ticket office from where he stood, but he could only make out one man inside, behind the counter.

"Stay here," he said. "I'll go check with the ticket clerk."

He left the boardwalk and crossed to mount the steps onto the platform, casting a glance along the street before he went inside. The office was just a tiny space in front of a waist-high counter, with two chairs and a spittoon for furniture. Behind the green-visored clerk he could see through a door into the little warehouse where the freight was stored.

The clerk said nobody fitting the description Slocum gave him had bought tickets anytime that week. "That don't mean nothing, though," he said. "A passenger can buy a ticket on the train. You don't have to have one to get on."

"When's the next train out?"

The clerk glanced at the big clock on the wall, which stood at 1:48. "Not for a couple hours yet. There's a train out south at five-ten. Another goes north at six-fifty. Won't be another for close to a week."

Slocum left the office and returned to where Red was lounging against the corner building. "No luck. But they can board without a ticket. Let's walk the town. Be best if we find them before the train gets here."

They spent the best part of the next two hours prowling the town, looking into saloons, checking shops and hotels and boardinghouses. It was a Saturday, a shopping day, and the town was crowded with people in from the surrounding countryside—cowhands, drovers, miners, prospectors, ranch wives stocking up for the week or the month. Once Red thought he saw Quinn going into a saloon, but when they eased their way in through the back entrance, the man turned out to be somebody else, a look-alike. Several times they made a detour in the street to get a look at a short busty woman under a flowered hat, but if Dory had acquired a flowered hat for disguise, she wasn't on the street. At a quarter to five they gave it up and headed back for the depot. If Dory and Quinn were planning to board that train they would have to come to the depot.

They approached it along the opposite side of the street this time, halting in an alley from which they could see across to the near end of the depot. The train hadn't arrived yet. The Indian woman was still hawking her wares in front of the ticket office, but there was no sign of the Mexican. A few passengers waited here and there on the end of the platform, but none of them looked familiar.

"I'm going to scout around the depot," Slocum said. "Quinn may be posted over there somewhere. If you see them before I do, don't try to take them yourself. Come a-running for me."

He left the shelter of the alley and started toward the near end of the platform. He took a hard look at the Indian woman as he approached—with her high cheekbones, Dory could maybe make herself up to look Indian, and that would be a smart ploy to throw off anybody looking for her—but the woman was definitely Indian, her black eyes dull with age. And the office was still empty except for the ticket clerk.

He went along the street side of the depot, keeping one eye on the traffic in the street. When he was sure

Quinn was not among the passersby, he mounted the side ramp up into the depot warehouse.

Boxes and barrels and bags of mail were stacked in the dim interior. The only light came from the ramp entrance he'd just come through and from the opening out onto the platform directly opposite. He put his back to the wall just inside the ramp entrance, one hand on his Colt, and let his eyes adjust to the dimness.

Two men wearing railroad caps were loading baggage onto a wheeled cart near the opposite entrance. Slocum waited till he had examined every dark corner of the room, then, certain that those two were the only men in the place, he crossed to tap one of them on the shoulder

"You seen a stranger in here anytime in the last hour or two? Young man with sandy hair? Looks like a gun hand?"

The man turned a sharp eye on him. "Nobody but railroad personnel allowed in here. Ain't seen nobody but you. If you're looking for somebody, look out on the platform."

Slocum restrained an impulse to teach the man how to give a civil answer to a simple question—he didn't have time for argument. He slipped out through the entrance onto the platform, edging up against the wall where he could see both ways along the building.

The Mexican was slumped against the wall to his left. Several other travelers were waiting along the platform, but none had the right look about them. There was still no sign of the train; the tracks stretched away empty toward the horizon. He sidled off along the platform to his right, toward the two freight wagons butted up against it.

He edged up to the corner of the depot and eased his head around it to check along the end wall. Nobody there. Nobody on the street that looked familiar. Across the street were two of the cheap saloons that straggled out from the end of town. He and Red had already checked them out. There wasn't time to do it again. If Dory and Quinn were waiting for the train there, he would have to take them when they came across to board.

He checked the two freight wagons. One of them contained a steamer trunk. The other was empty. He turned and made his way back along the platform.

The crowd of waiting passengers was growing; he looked hard at everyone he passed, but neither Dory nor Quinn was yet in evidence. He was beginning to get edgy; there was a stir in the crowd, people looking left along the tracks, and he saw the small black dot of the locomotive off on the horizon, approaching town, its plume of black smoke arching up from the stack. Wherever Dory and Quinn were, they had likely decided to cut it close, make a dash for the train just as it was pulling out. Unless Quinn was playing some sort of trick, disguising himself here among the crowd.

That Mexican, for instance. The right clothes and a sombrero pulled low could make even a blond-haired man look Mexican. Slocum sidled along the back of the crowd, loosening the Colt in his holster, angling over toward the Mexican.

The man was squatting against the wall, head and arms slumped down across his knees. Slocum could see no gun, but the serape draped over the man's shoulder would conceal one if he had it in his waistband. It wouldn't do to just make polite inquiry: Slocum headed for the man's legs, coming deliberately too close; his left boot kicked the man's feet from under him, and he wheeled and snatched the sombrero off as the man fell onto his side, uttering a Spanish oath.

It wasn't Quinn. The man had black hair and black eyes, looking up at Slocum with sleepy bewilderment. Slocum tossed him the sombrero. "Sorry, amigo," he said, and turned back toward the tracks.

He could hear the train now, coming closer, and see its plume of smoke above the heads of the crowd. A quick look told him Dory and Quinn still hadn't showed. The only place he hadn't looked was the cattle pens beyond that stretch of ground across the tracks, where there were two or three sheds they could be hiding in. The crowd was growing; they might slip into it from any number of places, but the train would put those sheds out of sight as soon as it pulled in.

Moving faster now, he jostled through the waiting passengers to signal to Red.

The train was only two hundred yards down the tracks when Red came trotting up onto the platform. Slocum grabbed him by the arm and worked him up to the edge of the crowd.

"I can't find them. You get on the other side of the tracks. Watch those sheds by the cattle pens, but don't lose sight of the train. Make sure they don't board from the other side."

Red jumped down off the platform and barely made it across the tracks before the locomotive pulled up even with Slocum, its big black bulk blocking out the cattle pens. Slocum felt the heat of it as it passed, chuffing slowly, the bell atop the boiler swinging wildly, its *ding-ding-ding* sharp above the belching of the engine and the rumble of the iron wheels. It pulled on past the end of the depot, bringing the first of its four Pullman cars even with the far end of the platform, and ground to a halt with a squeal of brakes and a hiss of steam.

As soon as it was stopped, Slocum grabbed a side rail and climbed the steps near the back end of the second car, where he could see the doors of the next one up the line. A conductor had dismounted and was holding back the waiting passengers while the others got off. Slocum was sure that Quinn and Dory weren't in the crowd; he glanced back along the train to where the last two cars stuck out beyond the end of the platform. The doors had remained closed on those; all passengers were dismounting through the first two. That meant two less cars to watch, but the caboose was back there—they migh' make a dash for the caboose, force their way inside till the train was out of the station. But Red should see them if they tried.

The waiting passengers were getting on now. Slocum kept one hand on his Colt, clinging to the side rail, feeling boarders brush by him, keeping his eyes on the doors up the train, on the dwindling crowd, on the onlookers milling around the depot. A horse-drawn buggy rushed up to the near end of the platform, a man and a woman inside, and Slocum swung off the steps, flattening himself against the car as the horse skidded to a halt and the man jumped out to help the woman down. But it wasn't them—the man was silver-haired, looking like a preacher in his black coat and hat, and the woman was old enough to be Dory's mother. Slocum hoisted himself onto the steps of the Pullman again, head up, scanning the doors ahead.

The last passenger got on. Half a dozen well-wishers remained on the platform, one or two waving to the friend or relative they were seeing off. The two railway clerks wheeled out a cart and loaded a mail sack on; the conductor clambered back onto the steps of the first car and shouted out the warning call to board.

Slocum swung down onto the platform, wanting something solid under his feet. This was maybe the moment they were waiting for; the engine was building up steam, the bell ringing again, the conductor leaning out to look up and down the length of the train. If they were going to catch it they would have to make the dash in the next few seconds. There was that train going out north at 6:50, but from everything he'd heard—from Boldt, from Red, from Dory herself—he was sure she was set on California, and south was the way to go for that.

The engine had begun to belch out smoke again; the conductor shouted out one last call to board, and the train began to inch away. Slocum stood where he was, the windows of the second car sliding past him, picking up speed; it was either now or they wouldn't make it, and he didn't think they could have boarded from the other side—Red would have seen them and kicked up a fuss; he would have heard that even above the hiss of steam. He turned back to watch the last car coming up toward the platform.

It was then that he saw Dory.

He was looking back through the length of the car as the first window came up to him. She was sitting in the last seat in the rear, across the aisle, a basket in her lap, looking out the opposite window. She was wearing a dress he hadn't seen before, its ruffled collar highlighting her face, and she had a hand to her mouth, one finger clutched between her teeth in a way that let him know she was frightened, that made her look like a girl again, like the little backwoods fifteen-year-old who used to sneak out of her daddy's house to meet him for night-swimming down by the river; and then the car pulled even with him, pulled past him, and he was running up the platform, knocking people aside, trying to stay even with the caboose as the train pulled away.

He dodged a woman waving to a friend, watched a railway clerk leap back out of his path, jumped the cart the mail sack had been wheeled out on, and he was almost to the end of the platform when somebody rushed him in a blur from the right, tackled him—and he went down.

He landed hard on his shoulder; he had his Colt out even as he fell, fighting to get free, but a hand grabbed his wrist and he was wrestled onto his back—through the sudden blur, he saw it was Quinn, blond hair hanging in his eyes, his young, almost too pretty face sweating from the strain, the cords standing out in his neck. Slocum bucked up to dislodge him, but Quinn slammed him back down, beating his gun hand against the platform, his voice almost desperate: "She said not to hurt you. Let it go. Let it go."

In his surprise, Slocum felt his grip slacken, felt the Colt knocked from his hand, and then Quinn was off him, on his feet and leaping off the platform after the train.

Slocum rolled onto his knees, coming to his feet to see Quinn running up the tracks after the caboose. He looked for his Colt, couldn't find it, jumped from the platform to find it lying in the dust. He scooped it up, leveled it at Quinn's fleeing back, watched the man straining to gain on the caboose—gaining, gaining, then reaching up to grab the rail above the rear steps and swing himself aboard.

For a moment, Slocum held the Colt at arm's length, centered on Quinn. Quinn stood on the caboose steps, looking back toward the depot, but he hadn't drawn his own gun. Then the caboose passed out of range, and Slocum lowered the Colt.

Red had come running from across the tracks. He had his gun out, and he was breathing hard. "Did you see her? She was on the train. Did you see her?"

"I saw her." Slocum holstered his Colt, watching the train pulling away, Quinn still standing on the caboose steps.

"She must have got on up the line. Must have flagged it down. They'd stop for a woman."

"Yes, and sent Quinn on here to watch for us. I'll say this for him. He did a good job."

The train was receding into the distance, the gleaming rails stretching away empty toward that rapidly dwindling dot where they seemed to merge. Slocum could no longer tell whether Quinn was still on the caboose steps or had talked his way inside. One long faint scream of the whistle drifted back with the trail of smoke from the engine—then Slocum turned to see Red watching his face, as if to judge what he was thinking.

"Do we go after 'em?" Red said.

He looked a little desperate, obviously waiting to be told what he wanted to hear, but whether that was to chase after Dory or to let her go, to finally let himself off her hook, Slocum couldn't tell. But this was the time to cut Red loose from her; catching up to her would only entangle him again. And likely Dory would need that money more than either he or Red did. She had picked a hard life to live, and like she'd said, she was getting a little old to start over at the bottom of it. So let her go, let her take that money and set herself up in business—she was shrewd enough to make it work. And that might be all she would have to help her through a lonely old age.

What was left of the crowd was watching them from the depot platform. Slocum figured they'd best get away from here before they had to answer a lot of questions. He touched Red on the arm. "Be a little hard to catch them now."

Red had holstered his Colt; he was looking off along the tracks, to where the train had disappeared from sight. "I guess you're right," he said, and something like relief passed across his face.

"Let's go find a good saloon," Slocum said. "We got time for a drink or two. Then we'll put you on that train going north. Put you on the road to Oregon."

25

They chose a saloon on the main business street, crowded and noisy and dim even with the light coming through the front windows. For a long time they drank in silence. Red didn't seem to want to talk, and Slocum was lost in his own thoughts, remembering Quinn looking back at him from the caboose, remembering the desperate look on that young, almost too pretty face as Quinn had hammered his Colt hand against the platform, remembering Quinn's last words before he had jumped to run for the train: "She said not to hurt you."

So there was still a little good in Dory Baker after all, still a little goodwill left from those nights back in Georgia when they were young; and he saw again the image of her alone in the last seat in the last car of the train, looking out the window, the basket in her lap, and he knew that that was the way he was always going to remember her: alone, and frightened, and looking like a girl again, heading off toward unknown country with a man who was too young for her and who likely wouldn't stick; off to make another try at living the life she wanted, a try likely doomed by the kind of woman she was, the kind of woman she always had been. But she would keep trying. The same thing that made it hard for her to hold a man, that strong tenacious will that drew to her only men like Red, whom she would eventually despise, would keep her fighting for what she wanted till she died.

"I can't understand that Quinn," Red said abruptly. "You know, when he jumped down off that platform, he was looking right at me. I'd started running when I saw Dory. I couldn't have been more than twenty yards away. I had my gun out—for all he knew, I was about to drop him where he stood. But he just looked at me, and then he took off after that caboose. I don't understand it."

"She told him not to hurt you," Slocum said.

"She what?"

"That's what he said. Right after he tackled me. He could have killed me, too, but that's what he said: 'She said not to hurt you.' "

He didn't know if that had applied to Red or only to himself, but there was no reason not to let him believe it was so. And from what Red had said, likely it was.

"Well, I'll be damned," Red said.

Slocum could guess the thoughts going through his mind, thoughts likely not too dissimilar to his own: of Dory at fifteen, back in Georgia in '65, and himself young then, too, and what life had done to them in between and what it still had waiting for them up the road.

"You know, you could have killed him, too," Red said "I saw you drawing down on him, and he was still in range."

"I didn't hear you shooting, Red. And it sounds like you had him nailed."

"You know, I couldn't. I had it in mind to, but I couldn't. I guess it was—well, I guess I didn't want to hurt her. If she wants him instead of me, why, I guess she's got a right to. God knows I haven't amounted to much. My daddy blames Dory for the road I took, but I was scouting the wrong side of the law before I ever followed her out here. I don't mean in Georgia. I figured that Yankee train we hit was just to make up for what Sherman's troops did to us. We got to Oregon, I aimed to settle right down. Only didn't seem like I could. Fell in with some boys, we got started stealing beef off a Indian reservation up there. Government beef, to feed the Indians. Didn't get caught at it, but we did it. Daddy never could abide Dory, but he can't hold my life against her.''

"You'll be home in a few days, Red. Your daddy'll be glad to have you back. You can talk all that out with him then.''

Red subsided into silence after that, sitting slumped over the bar and turning his glass in slow circles between his hands, watching the little wet rings it made on the bar top. Slocum found himself feeling uncomfortable, watching the clock above the bar and disliking himself for wanting to be gone—away from here, and away from Red. He didn't like to admit how unpleasant it was sitting next to an old friend and seeing clearly what a ruin he had become. When the clock said six-thirty, he downed the last of his drink and paid the bill.

"Time to go, Red.''

"Yeah," Red said, but he didn't look happy about it.

They were silent all the way to the train depot, Red slouching along with his thumbs hooked in his gun belt, watching the ground in front of his feet. The town had thinned out considerably; the treeless streets looked bleak in the late sun, and a muffled silence was settling in—the kind of quiet that came with evening, when the shops had closed and the outlyers had headed their wagons toward home and the townfolk had all gone in to supper. He could hear the train approaching in the distance, but the depot platform was empty save for a drummer with his case of wares. Not much call for traveling north.

Long evening shadows stretched along the platform; a clerk was waiting with a mail sack on a cart. "You got money for a ticket, Red?''

"I got a little. Enough to get home." Red nodded toward the ticket office and laughed. "Maybe I ought to get a ticket south.''

It wasn't much of a joke; the laugh was a little shaky, and there was something akin to fear on his face: fear that he might just do it—or fear of what life would be like if he didn't. Slocum thought how hard it must be to face things alone after seventeen years of sticking to one woman; every man needed an anchor to his life, and bad as she'd been to him, Dory had always been Red's.

He didn't want to think what that long trip home was going to be like, or how Red would take to it once he got there. Red loved his liquor a little too much, and it wouldn't be the first time he'd gone back to Oregon only to leave after a month or a year, off to look for Dory again. This time he likely wouldn't leave so long as his daddy was hanging on, and maybe his daddy's death would set him to thinking about his life—what he'd done with it, and what he was going to do with the rest of it. And maybe Ira, his brother, and Ira's family would find some way to hold him and settle him down.

The train puffed slowly into the station, inching past them in a haze of heat and steam and noise, the tall cars blocking off what remained of the sun. The engine wheezed to a stop; the conductor swung down to let one passenger off, and the clerk began loading the mail sack aboard.

Red turned to him, face squinted up in an effort to keep it under control. He thrust his hands in his back pockets, watched his boot toe dig at a nail head sticking up out of a board, then glanced off along the platform. "You think you'll ever get to Oregon again?"

"Hard to say, Red. I've covered a lot of country since we left Georgia. Don't usually know where I'm going to be. But I'll try to make it. Your brother Ira raises some good apples. We'll sit around under a tree drinking apple cider and talking over old times."

Red glanced at him and looked away again. "Sounds like a couple old men. Sitting around chewing up the past."

"Well, Red, there's worse ways to spend your days than sipping apple cider under a tree."

"I hate to think so, but I guess you're right. A man's got to face that sooner or later."

The mail sack was on board; the clerk was wheeling the cart back toward the warehouse entrance. Now the *ding-ding-ding* came from the little bell atop the engine, and the conductor swung up onto the steps of the first car. *"Booard. All abooard."*

Red turned to face him then, biting his lower lip, and stuck out his hand. "Well, Cap'n, I wish things had turned out better. Since we saw each other last, I mean. Kind of lost something after the war. I was a good soldier. You told me that once. A good Johnny Reb. Don't know what happened since, but I feel like I let the cause down."

Slocum shook his hand. "I'll be seeing you, Red. You better run, or you'll miss your train."

Red was only a few steps away when he turned again. "Cap'n? Cap'n, do me a favor, will you? You ever run in to Dory again—anywhere, to talk to, I mean—you tell her if she needs to, why, she can always come to Oregon. If I ain't there, Ira'll know where to find me. You tell her I'll be there if she needs me."

"I'll tell her, Red. If I see her, I'll tell her."

Red caught the handrail of the last car as it passed, swung up onto the steps, and turned to look back. The locomotive was building up speed, drawing its chain of cars out of the station, each one rocking a bit, clicking over the rails. Slocum followed along till he reached the end of the platform, then stopped and watched the train pull away, Red still clinging to the handrail. He could see the wind beginning to whip at Red's hat. Red took it off and raised it like a flag overhead, like a banner of still unbeaten defiance; he held it there for what seemed a long time, then he brought it down and disappeared up into the car.

Slocum turned and started back along the platform. The depot and the corrals and the dusty streets seemed very quiet after the noise of the train. He descended the platform steps and headed for the saloon he and Red had just left. He didn't think he could face a hotel room yet. Those cold walls always started him thinking about his life—what he'd done with it, and what he was going to do with the rest of it. He had a hunch tonight might be a little worse that way than most, and he wanted some good whiskey and bright lights and maybe a little soft talk with a woman first. Even a saloon woman could be an anchor for a time. For a night, anyway.

**GREAT WESTERN YARNS FROM ONE OF THE
BEST-SELLING WRITERS IN THE FIELD TODAY**

JAKE
LOGAN